THE FORBIDDEN

A MARDRAGGON NOVEL

By
SAWYER BENNETT

D1707790

Find Sawyer on the web!
sawyerbennett.com
twitter.com/bennettbooks
facebook.com/bennettbooks

Table of Contents

CHAPTER 1

Kat

THE RHYTHMIC SOUND of hooves striking the soft earth in the training arena accompanies my instructions. "Sit back in your saddle, Eliza."

I scrutinize the young rider post atop Bentley, one of Blackburn Farm's lesson horses. The morning sun filters through the open doors at the south end, throwing slivers of dappled light across the ground. Bentley tosses his head, ears pinned back as they approach, and he tries to decide how menacing those splotches of pale color may be. Saddlebreds are spirited horses and some even consider them a little crazy. Bentley's a good boy, but sometimes he gets easily spooked.

Which is what he does, skittering sideways to avoid the light and throwing Eliza slightly off balance.

The sudden motion from the big bay scares the young girl and she leans her body forward, a counterintuitive move that actually makes her less stable in the flat English saddle.

"You're fine," I say, my tone a mixture of discipline and calm instruction that horse training demands. "Get him back in a trot."

The girl straightens.

"Trot," she commands, and Bentley falls in line, his big head held high as he slips back into the cadence of alternately lifting each diagonal pair of legs. Eliza rises and falls in the saddle appropriately, bringing the gelding back under her command.

I stand in the center of the arena, my keen eyes observing every movement—the way she holds her hands, her posture, heels down and toes up—as Eliza guides Bentley around the edge, sticking close to the rail as she should.

"Good. Now bring him to a walk and two point," I say.

"Whoa," Eliza says with a slight pull on the reins and the horse slows. They plod along as Eliza stretches out of the saddle, legs straightening, body bent forward.

"One trip around and then you can bring him to his stall. Excellent ride."

Eliza grins because that's indeed high praise from me.

I start across the arena, intent on grabbing my water bottle. Eliza was my last lesson of the day and I'm looking forward to a long, hot shower. I haven't had a break yet except for a quick pee, and I'm starved.

My phone buzzes in the side pocket of my riding

jods and I pull it out. It's Ethan, asking me to come up to his office at the main house. Such a request would ordinarily annoy me at the end of long hours in the barn, but I've got an extra well of compassion for my oldest brother these days. He's been through so much lately that I'll be cutting him lots of slack for the foreseeable future.

"I'm heading up to the main house," I call out to Sara, one of the grooms waiting to help Eliza remove Bentley's tack.

"Got it all covered, Kat," she replies with a wave of her hand.

Outside of the training arena, I tip my face back to the May Kentucky sun and relish the late-afternoon warmth. The light hitting towering oaks casts long shadows across the verdant pastures, highlighting the vibrant greens of spring. The air is filled with the sweet scent of blooming wildflowers, freshly cut grass and bales of hay to feed the horses. It's the smell of my favorite time of the year and I relish this quiet moment of solace in the bustling life of Blackburn Farms.

I've been at the barn since six this morning, working on lesson plans and making sure the schedule of horses was ready. It's been a ten-hour day, which I'll repeat tomorrow, and I'll go to bed with a smile on my face because I'm doing what I love. Being a horse trainer is in my blood—I'm a Blackburn, after all—and our lineage has been producing and training the best saddlebreds in the world for over a hundred and seventy-five years, give or take a decade. This is what I was born to do.

My gaze sweeps over the rolling hills of our acreage, bordered by white rail fencing and dotted with grazing horses. In the distance, I can see the broodmare barn where Ethan has been burning the candle at both ends. This is his time of year… helping to bring into the world all the babies our breeding program produces, but that responsibility is just one of a million he has as the CEO of Blackburn Farms.

To add to his load, within the last six weeks, he learned he has a ten-year-old daughter he didn't know about—the product of a drunken one-night stand with Alaine Mardraggon—enemy to our family by virtue of her last name. Sylvie was born and raised in France and Ethan only found out about her after her mother Alaine died of cancer. Since then, it's been a bitter struggle with the Mardraggons over Sylvie's custody.

It culminated in an ending none of us saw coming when Lionel Mardraggon, Sylvie's grandfather, tried to kill her so he could assume control of the winery in France that Alaine left to her daughter. The thought of what that monster nearly did causes fury to well in me so hotly, I know I have the capacity to murder in defense of those I love. If Lionel Mardraggon were standing in front of me right now, I'd rip him apart with my bare hands.

He's a monster through and through.

As it stands, he's in jail, charged with attempted murder, and I'm going to have to let the justice system do its thing.

So, yeah… Ethan's been dealing with a lot and I'm happy to go up to the main house to see what he needs. I jump onto my Gator that I had custom painted in pink camo, a nod to my femininity that often gets overshadowed since I'm usually covered in horse hair and barn dust. I crank the motor and head off toward the main house, over a series of dirt and gravel paths that traverse the thousand acres of pastures, barns, training arenas and medical facilities that make up the Blackburn Farms enterprise.

Hundreds of horses and an army of grooms, stable hands, veterinarians, trainers, instructors and administrative staff, and Ethan is in charge of running it all. It's a task he took on when our parents, Fi and Tommy Blackburn, decided it was time to retire and hand over the literal and metaphorical reins.

I see my brother Trey at one of the yearling barns, directing a tractor trailer loaded with hay. He and my other brother Wade are also trainers, but we pitch in to help wherever we're needed. I expect Ethan asked Trey to oversee the deliveries today as he's got his hands full dealing with this Lionel Mardraggon mess and the fallout it has caused for our family, but most of all, for Sylvie.

The main house comes into view, a symbol of homecoming to me. I was raised here, although I currently live in an apartment above one of the tack rooms. My need for independence at the age of nineteen meant I left the big house eight years ago, although I still return for meals throughout the week. Only Ethan and Sylvie live there now. My parents occupy a cottage on the farm, and Trey and Wade share a house in Shelbyville.

I pull my Gator alongside Miranda's MINI Cooper. She's been our housekeeper and cook for over twenty years and, as expected, I find her in the kitchen working on this evening's meal. She's breading pork chops and my stomach rumbles because that's one of my favorite meals. She glances up as I walk in and gives me a pointed glare. "Boots off."

Grinning sheepishly, I unlace my boots and toe them off, grabbing an apple out of the basket on the counter as I walk by. "What else are we having tonight?"

"Green beans, roasted potatoes and creamed corn," she replies as she coats a chop in a seasoned blend of breadcrumbs and flour.

"Biscuits?"

"Sourdough rolls. I'm trying a new recipe."

I shoot her a wink. "It will be fabulous. Can't wait."

Taking a bite of the crisp red apple, I make my way out of the kitchen, down the hall to the parqueted main foyer, and right into Ethan's office. A portrait of our great-great-great-grandfather, Robert Blackburn, hangs behind the solid oak desk. He's the patriarch who built this house in 1902.

The office is a stark contrast to the barn—orderly, quiet, a place of decision and contemplation. Ethan looks as at home bent over paperwork as he does helping to deliver a breech foal. He's a man who can do it all and has my utmost respect on top of my undying love.

He looks up as I enter, his green eyes dulled with frustration, but he still manages a smile. "How was your day?"

I plop down in a chair opposite his desk. "Typical. Sixteen lessons. How was yours? You know, between managing an empire, birthing foals, dealing with a homicidal Mardraggon, and raising the cutest little girl east of the Mississippi."

Ethan's shoulders relax as he laughs, a rare moment of lightness breaking through his usual stoicism. "You mean the cutest little girl in the United States."

"Can't say," I reply, considering another bite of my apple. "I haven't been west of the Mississippi."

"Well, I have and it's time wasted," he mutters, pushing aside a stack of papers he'd been reading.

"You look tired," I say, a casual observation and not one meant as a put-down. I take a small bite of the apple.

Ethan rubs a hand over his stubbled jaw, his fingers lingering as if trying to soothe the weariness. He exhales slowly, the weight of countless restless nights reflected in his eyes. "Sleep hasn't been easy," he admits as he leans back in his chair, the leather creaking under his movement.

"How's the kiddo today?"

"She's good." I note that Ethan's voice doesn't sound strained, which means he's telling me the truth. "She's at Marcie's now."

Marcie is Sylvie's school principal, but more importantly, Ethan's girlfriend. I expect she'll be more than that one day, but she's been a godsend the last few weeks. Not only did she single-handedly help bridge the gap between Sylvie and our family—due to all the lies the Mardraggons had been feeding her—but Marcie has managed to bring out a softer side to my brother that I haven't seen before. Even with the weight of the world on his shoulders, for the first time I can recall, he's actually incredibly happy—despite the shit show going on in his life.

Guess love works a miracle now and then.

"Listen," Ethan says tentatively and picks up a spiral notebook. "I hate to ask this of you, but I was wondering if you might take over managing the medical on all the horses. Being in the middle of foaling season and then dealing with all this Lionel mess, and trying to figure out the winery business—"

"Say no more." I lean across the desk and grab the

notebook from him. "I've got it covered. What else can I do?"

"I don't know." He huffs, waving his hands at the stacks of papers strewn across the desktop. "I'm trying to parcel stuff out as I come across it."

I take in the tight lines on Ethan's handsome face. He has the same black hair and green eyes as I do.

Same as Trey, Wade, and my twin, Abby, all of us siblings bearing such a striking resemblance, no one had a doubt that Sylvie was Ethan's daughter when she showed up in court that day bearing the same raven hair and ferny eyes as ours.

"What's your biggest source of frustration?" I ask, setting the notebook aside and chomping on my apple again. I chew quickly and swallow just as fast to keep the conversation flowing.

"This fucking trust that Alaine left," he grumbles.

"That says you have to manage the winery with Gabe," I lament.

Ethan nods with a mirthless smile. "It galled me before, having to work with the scumbag, but now it makes my skin crawl knowing…"

His words trail off, but I can fill them in. Knowing that Gabe's father, Lionel, tried to kill Sylvie.

I shouldn't have to point it out, and I hate doing it because I can't stand Gabe Mardraggon either, yet I find myself saying, "But he is the one who turned his father into the police. We'd have never known what happened without him."

"Yeah, I know, and I hate to give the bastard credit, but it still doesn't mean I have to like working with him."

I'd hate to work with the asshole too, but that doesn't stop me from saying, "Let me handle all the winery stuff with Gabe."

Ethan snorts, leaning forward in his chair. "I wouldn't wish that on my worst enemy." He seems pensive, then laughs at an internal joke. "Although I bet Wade and Trey would kill to have the opportunity to go after him."

"They'd kill him and then rot in jail with Lionel," I drawl. I consider another bite of my apple, but toss it into Ethan's garbage can at the side of his desk. "I'm serious. I'll handle Gabe Mardraggon. I'd kind of relish being a thorn in his side."

Ethan blinks as if he's just hearing my offer for the first time. "What? No! I couldn't ask you to do that. I can't stand to be in the same room with him, so I'm not about to put my baby sister in that position."

I glare at my brother. "I might be your baby sister, but I'm a capable woman, tough as nails and not about to let some snot-nosed Mardraggon cause havoc for our family. I can handle this for you."

Ethan's face is inscrutable, his thoughts a mystery as

he strokes his chin. "You don't know anything about running a winery."

"Neither do you," I point out. "But at the very least, I can be the go-between. Let me be the one to liaise with Gabe and I'll pass information back and forth for you to make decisions. I can totally handle that jerk."

"No doubt you can," Ethan muses but still doesn't accept my offer. His reluctance to interact with Gabe is understandable. Although he might be completely innocent in Lionel's plot to kill his own granddaughter, he's still a Mardraggon, and that's a hard pill for any Blackburn to swallow.

I wait out Ethan's decision, prepared to argue further with him if he's not hip to the idea. I have as much reason as anyone in our family to hate Gabe Mardraggon, but I can put that aside to help Ethan. He and Sylvie are the ones who matter.

After a long silence, he finally says, "Okay. I'll let him know that I don't have time to handle the winery stuff and you'll be acting in my stead, but keep me informed. Every step of the way."

"Every step," I assure him.

Ethan leans to the side, pulls open a deep desk drawer and flips through some folders. He pulls one out and hands it to me. "That's the trust agreement and basic financials that Gabe sent over. He's pushing to do some expansion and needs my agreement to move forward. I don't know if the deals are good or bad, but I want to do what's best for Sylvie's interests. Hear what he has to say and then we can discuss what to do."

I'm slightly intimidated taking the thick folder from him, feeling the weight of my new duties. I didn't finish college and don't have the same business savvy that Ethan does. I'm a horse trainer, although I think I'm fairly intelligent.

Ethan must sense my uncertainty. "You don't have to make any decisions, Kat. Just be my mouthpiece."

I nod, taking the folder and putting on a bright smile. "I've got it handled. Like I said... if I can make Gabe's life hell while doing this, that's just a bonus." I stand from the chair. "Now, I'm going to grab a shower before dinner."

"Sounds good," he says, his attention dropping back to his stack of papers.

I head out of his office but stop in the doorway, turning back to my brother. "Are you going to let Sylvie see Gabe at all?"

Ethan's countenance is troubled as he lifts his head. "Not right now. Even though Gabe is the one who turned in his dad, what if he had something to do with the plot? I mean... what if he was in on it and turned in his dad just so he could take control of the Mardraggon empire?"

Something to consider. The winery aside, the

Mardraggons are known for their Kentucky bourbon. Even as successful as the Blackburns are, we don't have the type of wealth the Mardraggons have, and they made it all on the amber liquid aged in oak barrels in the heart of Kentucky.

As much as I despise Gabe Mardraggon, I can't see him being involved in a plot to kill Sylvie. I truly believe he loves his niece, but I can't lose sight of the fact that he comes from a long line of cheating, lying and stealing assholes. The past clings to the present like a stubborn stain, the whispers of the original feud between our families coloring our lives in shades of bitterness and hate.

It's not only the very distant past that has me despising Gabe but more current events that have given me a firsthand view of just how despicable the man is.

Ethan's phone rings, pulling his attention. I give him a wave as I leave his office, my mind racing. I've had little interaction with Gabe since... well, since my freshman year of college. The few times we've run into each other have been an exchange of acerbic words and hate-filled stares. I'll never admit it aloud—the thought of dealing with him churns a tumultuous mix of dread and... something else—but I remind myself I'm not the starry-eyed girl I was when I went off to college.

And Gabe Mardraggon is nothing more than a spoiled, wealthy heir trying to control things because power makes him feel good. He's pathetic, really, and with that thought, I'm emboldened.

Working with Gabe will be a challenge, but I'm a Blackburn. Challenges are what we thrive on.

In the back of my mind, a voice whispers that this is more than just a business arrangement. It's a dance on a tightrope strung between past and present, hatred and something dangerously close to fascination.

CHAPTER 2

Gabe

THE STARK MODERNITY of my parents' contemporary mansion echoes the chill of their affection—or lack thereof. I didn't live here by choice or necessity but rather by lack of caring to live anywhere else. The twenty-two-thousand-square-foot abode ensured I could have complete sanctuary from their icy influence but all that space feels suffocating now.

I can't really bemoan the gilded cage I grew up in or the fact that my parents were emotionally absent from my and Alaine's lives. My father, Lionel, was always at the helm of our bourbon empire and my mother, Rosemund, was always at the country club drowning her woes in dirty martinis. But that was the only life I knew and it never felt lacking to me in all the years I've been alive. Many people consider me as cold as my parents and they wouldn't be wrong.

Even now, I don't think I've missed out on anything, but it feels wrong staying here. The halls are tainted with

Lionel's treachery and I'm drowning in guilt by association because of what he did to Sylvie. I might be a hard-hearted bastard but if there is one person on this earth who owns whatever softness hides within me, it's my niece.

How can I stay in this place when it shelters such betrayal? Such downright evil?

Rosemund's voice cuts through the air, sharp and unyielding as I head toward the front door, a designer leather duffel bag in hand. I'll send someone else for the rest of my bags but for now, it's enough to make my escape. "Gabe, you cannot be serious. Leaving now is madness—abandoning your father when he needs us most."

I set my bag down, adjust the cuff of my custom Italian suit and face my mother. "You mean sticking by the man who tried to kill his own granddaughter for profit? That's where you set the line of family loyalty?"

She bristles, her facade of perfection trembling as her mouth presses into a flat line. "We are Mardraggons. We stand together."

"Not this time," I growl, my resolve as solid as the gray marble floor I stand on. "Not after what he did."

"Your father is innocent. His attorney said all they have is circumstantial evidence. It's why he was granted bail."

I grimace at the reminder he's getting out of jail and

will, in fact, be arriving here within the hour. It's why I'm not delaying my exit. The judge was moved by dad's attorney enough to grant bail for a million dollars, forfeiture of his passport, and house arrest outside of work hours until his trial.

"This is all your fault," she hisses as she takes a step toward me, her gray eyes chilly with blame. "He wouldn't be in this predicament had you kept your mouth shut."

I've not had this out yet with my mom and it takes hardly anything at all for me to lose my shit. I glare at her, my voice dripping with scorn. "He tried to kill Sylvie. Your own flesh and blood. Alaine's daughter. How can you stand by his side?"

"He did not," she asserts, her voice sharp as she sniffs disdainfully. Her chin lifts, a clear gesture of defiance and dismissal. Her eyes, cold and calculating, lock onto me. "And we cannot afford to have this scandal hanging over us. The future of our company depends on these charges going away. So, we need to rally—"

I erupt with laughter, my head tilting as genuine but dark amusement overtakes me. I fix my gaze on hers, unblinking and piercing. "Oh, I see what's really going on here. You're afraid of all this going away. Your cushy lifestyle being swept out from under you."

It's a legitimate worry to have and she snaps her mouth shut because she knows I'm right. Rosemund does not love Lionel, nor does he love her. But she does love this lifestyle and he does love having a woman who will do his bidding no matter what.

I'm not about to let this company falter. I've called an emergency meeting of the board of directors and I've got plans of my own that will ensure the Mardraggon empire will continue to flourish. I don't share that with her though.

Bending over, I grab the duffel and pivot away from my mother. As I swing open the left side of the double doors, her voice cuts through. "Where are you going?"

"Far away from here," I mutter and step out onto the flat portico that's as austere as the rest of the house. All gray concrete and boxwood bushes trimmed with such precision, you could cut yourself on a corner. I always appreciated the clean lines and lack of frills but again… it all somehow seems wrong now and I'm not sure why.

I only know I've got to get the fuck out of here.

I leave Rosemund watching me with condemnation as I stalk toward the sleek red Ferrari SF90 Spider. Seven hundred and sixty-nine horsepower that I often take advantage of on Kentucky's winding back roads and I didn't blink an eye at the $580,000 price tag.

I toss the duffel in the passenger seat, rev the engine and peel out of the driveway, hoping the speed by which I exit is further proof to my mother that I can't get away fast enough.

Leaving all the poison behind.

It's guilt you're leaving behind, Gabe.

That thought comes unbidden and I push it away. I will not feel guilty about what I did to my father. He brought that upon himself.

But what if he didn't give her penicillin? What if Sylvie really has a heart condition or some other medical unknown that caused her to nearly die almost a week ago? The doctors didn't test her for penicillin poisoning at first, and the only proof the police have is the prescription pad I found in my father's office that had the faint imprint of what looked to be a prescription written for penicillin, but even that is dubious.

On the other hand, the police told me that it's more than just finding the prescription pad in his office. Lionel knew she had an allergy to the drug and it was damning that he would inherit the winery if she died. Couple that with the fact the prescription was written just three days before Sylvie came to stay the night and it was filled at a local pharmacy, Lionel was arrested because the circumstantial evidence was overwhelming.

Still… it was just circumstantial. No one saw him dose her.

But you know he did it, my subconscience pokes at me.

I pound on the steering wheel in frustration. I can't let these doubts surface. What's done is done and I have to trust that justice will prevail. If my father is innocent, then the truth will out. That's all I can hope for.

But until such time, I'm moving on with my life and my main priority is to keep Mardraggon Enterprises prospering and profitable.

I glance at my wrist, eyeing the sleek Patek Phillipe that circles it—a timepiece I snagged for just half what this car cost. The watch's elegant face, framed by a polished gold bezel, marks me fifteen minutes behind schedule for my appointment. Even though I'm used to people catering to me—I'm a Mardraggon, after all—I don't like to be late. It's bad business, so I put a quick call into the Realtor and let her know of my delay. She assures me it's fine as I drive the ten miles deeper into Shelby County, past saddlebred and thoroughbred farms.

While I guide the Ferrari past undulating hills, the heated conversation with Ethan Blackburn from this morning replays in my head like a bad track stuck on a loop. I'd received a cryptic email from him two days ago, telling me he doesn't have time to devote to the winery business and that he's going to have his sister, Kat, work on it. While Ethan will make joint decisions with me on big items, he's going to rely on Kat to serve as his liaison because he's simply too busy with "other things."

I called bullshit on that. It's clear that Ethan is creating a divide he won't let me cross. Not that I want to get any closer to him, but Sylvie stands on the other side of the chasm with him and I would very much like to see my niece.

I called him four times in a desperate attempt to bridge the distance that the feud and my father's heinous actions have created, and the fucker finally deigned to call me back this morning.

The first order of business was to nip his insane idea to have me deal with Kat on the winery. "I'm not dealing with your sister. She's a horse trainer, not a businessperson."

"She's smart as hell," Ethan retorted sharply and while I actually know this about Kat, I'm not about to validate it. "But she won't be making decisions. Just taking some of the workload off me."

I don't want to deal with Kat. She will be a royal pain in my ass and a distraction I don't need. In the end, I have no choice because Ethan said, "Deal with her or you'll have to wait until I'm in a position when I have time."

I suppose it is plausible he's just too busy but then the next part of the conversation devolved quickly—and that's how I know he's avoiding me.

"I would like to see Sylvie," I requested politely.

"Not going to happen," Ethan replied, the razor edge to his tone telling me I'd hit directly on his reticence.

"She's my niece," I stated evenly. "I love her."

"Your father tried to kill her," Ethan barked.

"And I turned him into the police," I grit out. Ethan remained silent, so I plunged forward. "I'm moving out of their house today. Sylvie has to be very confused, Ethan. She needs to hear the truth from me. She has to understand I was not a part of that and I've broken ties with my parents."

Ethan's voice conveyed a blend of irritation and defeat. "She knows you turned your father in, Gabe. But that doesn't change the fact that she needs space from all Mardraggons right now."

"For how long?" I asked, knowing I couldn't do a damn thing but abide by whatever he said.

"Until she's ready. It's not just me who has a problem with your family. Sylvie is scared. It's going to take some time."

"Is she seeing someone? A counselor or therapist?" I'm not a big believer in therapy. I navigated my family's dysfunction by hardening myself. But Sylvie still has a chance at a normal life, despite the horrors she's been through.

"Yes, she is. And she's working through things."

"I'm willing to go to therapy with her," I proposed earnestly. "You can be there too. Or at least let me see her in your presence."

"When she's ready," Ethan says, and then adds, "and maybe not even then. I have to be sure about things too and I don't know if the police have cleared you."

Hell, I didn't even know if the police had cleared me yet. They'd swept through the Mardraggon mansion with search warrants and crime scene technicians, pulling out boxes of documents, every computer, tablet and phone in the house. I knew they'd find nothing tying me to any plot to kill Sylvie, but I guess until they officially clear me to Ethan, I won't be getting anywhere near my niece.

"Kat will reach out to you to go over the winery stuff," Ethan said. "Make sure you treat her with respect."

"Or else you'll kick my ass?" I taunted.

"Don't have time," he replied with a snide laugh. "But I'll send Trey and Wade out to do it. Although now that I think about it, Kat's more than capable of handing you your own ass."

Didn't I know that firsthand?

The conversation ended, but his words lingered, stoking the fire of my determination. I won't let my father's sins screw the future I'm trying to build—for Sylvie, for the winery, for me. I press the accelerator, the engine's roar a defiant cry against blacktop roads.

When I pull up to the house that was just listed for sale three days ago, I don't give it much of a once-over. I've driven by this estate hundreds of times in my life and have always admired the sprawling sixty-two acres that house a seventeen-thousand-square-foot mansion complete with ten bedrooms and eighteen baths, a separate indoor pool house that's another thirteen thousand square feet, a detached ten-car garage, an eighteen stall barn and four ponds.

It is far more than one man needs, but if there's one thing the Mardraggons know how to do just as well as making money, that's spending it. The seven-and-a-half-million-dollar price tag is a bargain, considering the home comes fully furnished.

Jeanette Littleton walks down the porch steps wearing a bloodred skirt suit with black pegged heels. Her hair and makeup have been done to perfection, her long nails the color of her outfit. We exchange greetings and she coolly sweeps her hand toward the front door. "Shall I give you the tour?"

I nod and follow her inside, blown away by the opulence that wasn't quite translated by the pictures in the official listing.

The entry foyer is an architectural marvel with a grand staircase creating an elegant focal point as it curves gracefully upward. The glossy checkered marble floor reflects the natural light pouring through the floor-to-ceiling windows that offer an uninterrupted view of the estate's lush grounds.

Beyond the foyer is a luxurious living space, the grandeur amplified by towering columns and a striking mezzanine balcony under which sits a grand piano on a raised dais. Sumptuous armchairs and a sleek glass table suggest a blend of modern comfort with classic style, more suited to my personal tastes.

Jeanette leads me through the house, each room grander than the last. The master suite is a room unlike any I've ever seen and I've stayed at some of the finest hotels in the world and some of the most expensive homes of billionaire friends. Nothing compares to this lavish space. A four-poster bed anchors the room, surrounded by plump chairs you can sink down into and gleaming rich hardwood floors. Overhead, the ceiling features an intricate coffered design and skylights flood the space with natural light.

More floor-to-ceiling windows framed by crisp plantation shutters maintain the estate's southern vibe. The color palette is soft and natural with creamy whites, which are a welcome change to the dull gray of the Mardraggon estate. Every detail, from the ornate chandelier to the delicate floral arrangements, speaks to me on a softer level.

I'm taken on a golf cart tour of the acreage, over to the pool house and the barns but truly, I'd made my decision before we left the master suite.

At the conclusion of the tour, I tell Jeanette, "I'll take it."

"What would you like to counter at?" she asks, pulling out her iPad to make some notes. "And do you want any concessions?"

"I'll pay the asking price but I want to move in to-day. I'll gladly pay rent until we can close and I'll be paying cash."

The real estate agent blinks, stunned at the easy deal. "If that's the case, we can close fairly quickly."

"Make it happen," I instruct, and then I'm heading back to my Ferrari to drive into Frankfort where Mardraggon Enterprises are headquartered. Got more important business to attend to.

CHAPTER 3

Kat

HUSTLING THROUGH MY shower, I ignore the rumbling in my belly. I haven't eaten since breakfast because I've been going at a hundred miles an hour since I woke up at five a.m. I'm already bemoaning the fact I won't be joining the family tonight for some of Miranda's amazing meatloaf and mashed potatoes.

Agreeing to help Ethan with the medical management of the show horses was far more work than I'd anticipated, and I did a horrible job of planning out my day. Trying to manage the training schedule, actually training horses and giving lessons, and the host of administrative complications that come with it is a full-time job in and of itself. Add on the nightmare of managing the more than three hundred horses between the broodmares, foals, yearlings, studs, show horses, lesson horses and retired horses, it's enough to make my eyes cross.

What I learned today is that I can't bounce back and

forth between the two. I tried to pour through the countless spreadsheets that track routine vet visits, supplements and vitamins, chiropractic appointments, floating teeth and other illnesses in between training and lessons, and it was a disaster. I learned today that I'm not a multitasker of any great magnitude so my game plan on how to manage my day has changed.

Before leaving the barn today, I worked out a feasible schedule to compress my training lessons and hand off some to the other instructors. I then opened up my afternoons to be able to work on all the administrative stuff, including the medical management. I vowed I would do that here in my apartment so I wouldn't get distracted by the horses or the slew of people who are in and out of the barns each day. When it's all said and done, I'm proud of myself for figuring this out. It's vital that I'm able to help Ethan. Even if I have to put in twenty-hour days and sleep only four, I'll do my part to take the burden off his shoulders.

And it's with utter resolve and determination to include the unpleasant necessity of having to deal with Gabriel Mardraggon.

I'm already soured to our upcoming meeting this evening because his unwillingness to meet during the day means I'm missing Miranda's meatloaf. I've been trying for three days to force a meeting, but it seems he's as reluctant to work with me as I am with him.

Can't say I blame either one of us, given our history.

After my shower, I work at breakneck speed to dry my hair enough that I can put it in a messy topknot. I don't bother with makeup because I'm not trying to impress anyone and I slip into my favorite jeans before tugging on a Blackburn Farms T-shirt and a worn pair of Adidas. I glance at myself in the closet's full-length mirror, smirking as I think of the contrast between my casual comfort and someone like Gabe Mardraggon who dresses in only the finest designer clothing. I suppose if I made an effort to dress nicer, he might see me as more professional, but I really don't give a rat's ass what he thinks of me. I'll never care about that.

Glancing at my watch, I realize I've got enough time that I can probably swing through a drive-through for a hamburger on my way to see the Mardraggon. Nowhere near on par with Miranda's cooking but at least my stomach won't be threatening to eat itself.

I snag my keys, phone and purse before heading to the door. I switch off a tasseled lamp as I move past it, crossing the entire space in about ten steps.

My abode is small but full of charm and I can't imagine living anywhere else. Yes, I live above the main tack room next to one of the training barns but this place is wholly mine, not only in possession but in character. I've spent time over the years upgrading and decorating the place, mostly by myself, but sometimes with Trey and

Wade helping out with the heavier lifting. The walls are beadboard, painted a soft cream that contrasts beautifully with the natural wood beams that stretch across the ceiling. A squishy, deep-blue sofa adorned with throw pillows featuring horse motifs is the focal point of the living area which is only big enough to hold said couch. There's a small, antique coffee table overloaded with *The Saddle Horse Report* and *National Horseman* that I really need to clean out.

Adjacent to the living room is the kitchen, separated by a breakfast bar made from reclaimed barn wood that Trey and Wade helped me install. The kitchen is practical yet charming, with open shelving that holds mismatched plates and cooking pots above the compact, four-burner stove.

My bedroom sits on the other side of a sliding barn door, reclaimed from one of our yearling barns that we renovated a few years ago. The space is so small it only fits my queen-size wrought-iron frame and one tiny wooden nightstand with a vintage coin glass lamp with a beaded shade.

It's cozy but perfect for me.

When I throw open the front door, pausing to pat my back pocket to make sure I do indeed have my phone, even though I know in my head I picked it up just seconds ago, I'm brought up short by Sylvie standing on my stoop at the top of the wooden staircase. Her right hand is raised as if poised to knock.

She gives a startled yelp and then a sheepish grin. "You scared me."

Laughing, I press my hand to my own beating heart. "Ditto. What's up, kiddo?"

Her smile falters a tiny bit. "Can we talk?"

I don't glance at my watch or try to calculate how this will cause me to miss a swing through a fast-food joint or even possibly be late to my meeting. I only see my niece, who I've known for just a handful of weeks but for whom I would lay down my life.

Brave, sweet Sylvie who has the weight of the world evident in her eyes but is still trying to keep my worry at bay by projecting a shining smile.

"Of course. Come in." She slides by me and I set my purse, phone and keys on the kitchen counter. Sylvie moves to the blue couch and settles in. We've had a few movie nights here and I'm happy to see she's comfortable in my place. I didn't know I was born to be a doting aunt until I became one. I plop down on the opposite end, throw my arm over the back. "How was school today?"

I know she came here to talk about something specific but figured a little chitchat would be good. Today was her second day back as Ethan kept her out all of last week. Not only did he want Sylvie to have some more rest after her overnight hospital stay necessitated by the allergic reaction after her grandfather intentionally dosed her with penicillin, but Ethan knew the town would be rife with gossip following Lionel's arrest. He wanted Sylvie to have time to settle into the notion that her grandfather is a very bad, evil man and people are going to be extremely interested in following this developing story.

Sylvie lifts a shoulder. "It was fine. I mean… most of the kids were nice but a few were assholes."

God, she's so cute cursing with her sweet French accent. I don't chastise her. I'm the cool aunt who lets her get away with that stuff when times are tough and she's been swept up in a shit show. Six weeks ago, her mother died. Five weeks ago, she came to live with Ethan, the father she'd never met, and with him, she inherited the motley Blackburn lot. It's been a difficult adjustment, but Sylvie is starting to flourish. Then, ten days ago, her own grandfather tried to kill her, all so he could gain control of the winery his daughter Alaine had left to her daughter.

My inclination is to pull Sylvie into my arms to comfort her, but she looks at me with pleading eyes, not to help her fracture but to be strong. "Bullies feed on reactions, my dear sweet niece. Starve them of it, and they lose their power."

She considers my words and nods. "I know." She then lifts her chin. "It doesn't bother me."

"That's my warrior girl," I praise.

"Much," she adds on. "It doesn't bother me much."

"You wouldn't be human if it didn't affect you in some way."

Her gaze drops to her hands and I know she wants to get to the heart of the matter, the reason she sought me out. When it comes, I'm not prepared for it.

Her green eyes—same as Ethan's, same as mine, same as all my siblings and my sweet Irish mom—rise to meet mine. "I know you're going to see Gabe. I overheard you and Dad talking."

"Oh," I murmur, mind racing to the conversations I've had with Ethan the last few days about this meeting with Gabe and whether we specifically talked about Sylvie, or rather… Sylvie and Gabe's relationship.

"I was wondering how he is."

"How who is?" I ask, not trying to play dumb but to give myself more time to make sure I will say the right things. Gabe is dangerous territory to discuss.

Sylvie rolls her eyes, knowing I'm being deliberately obtuse. "I want to know how Uncle Gabe is. I want to see him."

"Oh, wow. Um… okay, that's not up to me, kiddo. That's your dad's call."

"I know," she huffs, crossing her arms over her chest and settling back against the cushion. "He doesn't want me to see him, but I thought maybe you could talk to my dad. And since you're going to be seeing my uncle today, I was hoping you could… you know… let him know that I don't blame him."

I ignore that for the moment. "Honey… have you really talked to your dad about this? Does he know how you feel?"

She shakes her head. "I only asked once but he's got a lot of worries on him. I don't think he wants to hear that I want to see Uncle Gabe because he hates the Mardraggons so much."

"He's just protecting you."

Sylvie's face screws up with frustration. "Yes, I know. But I don't believe Gabe had anything to do with it. Do you?"

I can't tell Sylvie that I probably know Gabriel Mardraggon better than any Blackburn does, including herself, and while what I know gives me far more reason to despise him than any of the others, I truly can't see him being involved in a plot to kill Sylvie. I know he was close to Alaine. I know he loves Sylvie.

I shake my head. "No, I don't think Gabe had any idea Lionel was going to do that. But it's very complicated, Sylvie. That's his father and he will be loyal to his family. Maybe not to Lionel in particular but to the Mardraggon name. Gabe's interest in protecting that worries your dad."

"But Uncle Gabe wouldn't hurt me," Sylvie insists,

and my heart constricts painfully as I see how tortured she is about this. "He's the last tie to my mother."

"I know," I murmur, reaching over to rest my hand on her shoulder. "Tell you what… I'll talk to your dad after I meet with Gabe, okay? We'll try to figure out something."

"And you'll tell Uncle Gabe I don't blame him?" she presses.

"Of course I will. In fact, would you like to write him a note and I'll give it to him?"

Sylvie's eyes light up and she nods exuberantly. "Yes, that would be awesome."

I have no clue if Ethan would approve of this, and I fully intend to let him know what I'm doing.

But after I hand the note over.

This is important to Sylvie and I'll take the heat if it pisses Ethan off. But at this point, I can't see the harm in making her feel good about maintaining the hope of a relationship with the one person who loved her mother the way she did.

CHAPTER 4

Gabe

THE OFFICE IN this new house was also a major selling point for me. It doubles as a library, stocked with shelves upon shelves of classic books bound in rich, brown leather. It's not that I'm an avid reader, although I do read on occasion, but it's the room's atmosphere that speaks to me. White paneled walls, fabric-draped windows and dark hardwood floors softened by a deep blue and white geometric-patterned rug underfoot gives me the warmth and casual comfort I never had at my parents' home. A buttery caramel leather couch sits before a hand-carved mantel, also in white, and the cherry desk is ornate and old-fashioned.

It's traditional and charming, the absolute antithesis to the minimalist décor and concrete gray walls of the Mardraggon estate that screamed of order and strict boundaries.

In the early twilight, the moss-covered oaks and the edge of the pool house are visible outside the panoramic windows with a hint of horse pasture beyond, but those fields are empty. I'm not a horse person nor did I buy this estate to fill it with such. I don't appreciate the scenery and only spare it a glance before focusing on the thick sheaf of papers before me. I'm three hours deep into plotting the careful dismantling of Lionel Mardraggon's legacy. I plan to remove him from the head of our empire.

A knock pulls me from my thoughts and I'd nearly forgotten I had an appointment this evening.

It's her—Kat Blackburn—and I'm immediately tense with anticipation of a fight.

I've put off this meeting as long as possible. Just days ago, I was hounding Ethan to meet with me because we have some major business decisions to make about the winery and I can't make a move without his approval. But now that Ethan has delegated his duties to his sister, I don't want to be bothered with any of it.

Okay, that's not quite accurate.

It's Kat I don't want to be bothered with.

Of all the Blackburns I would've preferred to deal with on a business matter, Kat would be the last. She's the least preferable to have to pass on opposite sides of a busy street because even that close of a proximity invites disgruntlement.

It's always been that way, some occasions stronger than others, and it will never change.

But as it stands, if I want to have a pathway back to Sylvie, it seems the winery is my best chance. Therefore, I'm going to have to deal with the raven-haired beauty.

When I open the front door, she stands there in all her perfect glory, her green eyes burning promises of mayhem as they pierce me. She's a horse girl through and through and always has been. Although I've seen her at high-society functions in dazzling gowns, Kat Blackburn is most comfortable—and admittedly, most beautiful— in faded jeans, her face scrubbed free of makeup. She's got a purse over one shoulder and a three-ring binder tucked under her arm.

"You're late," I say, having glanced at my watch on the way to greet her, even though I lost track of time myself. I don't let her know that.

"Tough shit," she replies as she pushes past me into the house.

"Come on in," I mutter with an exaggerated sweep of my hand from behind her while shutting the door.

Tucking my hands into my pockets, I watch as Kat's head tips and she takes in the cathedral ceilings with coffered beams. The heavy chandeliers are dimmed and cast a warm glow on the parquet floors. Another selling point of the house—the softness of the lighting.

She glances back at me. "Could you have picked anything more ostentatious? What do you need all this for?"

I shrug, the corner of my mouth quirking. "What's the point of having money if you're not willing to spend it?"

"Spoken like a true shyster of a Mardraggon," she purrs.

"Spoken like a snot-nosed Blackburn brat," I retort.

"Better a brat than a murd—"

"Careful, Hell Kat," I warn in a low growl. "You can throw venom all you want at me, but don't you dare put me in the same category as my father."

Those green eyes flash with ire that I stopped her tirade but I see something deep within that she probably doesn't want to concede to me.

Contrition.

But she wants the last word, so she waves a dismissive hand. "This house is over the top and you know it."

"Sorry if I don't relish living in barns and smelling like horseshit," I drawl with a slow rake of my eyes down her body.

I'm not sure what it says about me when her cheeks flush red and those eyes light up with something close to hellfire, and it looks like she could happily punch me. Instead, she takes a long step and leans in close, whispering, "I just took a shower, so I know I smell good."

Fuck if my lungs don't betray me, my nostrils flaring just so I can be proven wrong. Yeah… she smells like spring flowers and spicy citrus.

I never want her to know that I need space from all that she represents so I turn on my heel and head toward my office. "Might as well get this over with," I say brusquely.

She's whisper quiet behind me but I can feel her presence as she follows. To keep things professional, I take a seat behind my desk and point to a chair on the opposite side. She settles into it, dropping her purse to the floor and placing the binder on her lap.

Kat glances around the office, eyeing the bookshelves with interest before her gaze settles on me. "So, really… what's the deal? Why did you move out of your parents' mausoleum?" She inclines her head in faux apology. "I'm sorry. I mean home. Did you buy this monstrosity because you're trying to compensate for something?"

I'm not sure why she needs to keep making her digs but I suspect it's just to get a rise out of me. I decide to quell it quickly. "You of all people know I don't need to compensate."

I hold my breath, waiting for her to explode with rage. I can feel the air crackle between us, the undeniable tension that speaks of a shared past that neither of us dare acknowledge.

But she breaks it by smiling, scoffing with amusement before her expression turns hard and unyielding. She holds up the binder. "I read the trust agreement and the other financials. I'm ready to discuss the winery."

"And like I told you when you reached out to me, we don't need to do anything right now. This meeting could have waited."

Which isn't exactly true. There are things we need to move on but I didn't want to deal with her and was hoping Ethan would come around and deal with me himself.

"Yet you were so eager to talk to Ethan," she counters with narrowed eyes.

No sense in lying. "Because I wanted to have a way in to see Sylvie."

She's unfazed by my proclamation and ignores it, probably to piss me off. "No, you told my brother that decisions had to be made regarding expansion plans. So I'm curious why you're avoiding it? Is it because you have to deal with me?"

Chuckling, I steeple my fingers, appraising her a moment. "You're no peach to deal with, Hell Kat."

She glares at me. "Stop calling me that."

"Why?" I probe, feeling like I have the upper hand for a change and enjoying the leverage. "You used to like it."

"That was a long time ago," she says primly, her voice a cool brush-off that doesn't quite reach her eyes. There's defiance in her words, challenge in her eyes. And for a moment, I remember why she's so attractive beyond her physical beauty.

Because she was unattainable in all ways and that only makes something more desirable. But as she said, that was a long time ago.

"Look," I say, giving a pointed glance at the binder in her hand. "You need to review more than a few profit-and-loss statements to be able to talk intelligently about the winery."

"How about you just lay it out to me like I'm a fifth grader and I'll pass it on to Ethan," she replies coolly.

"Fine." I lean forward in my chair, clasp my hands on the desk. "We have a major investment opportunity which will expand the wine distribution network. There are some innovative but risky marketing strategies I'd like to implement. Each decision could significantly impact revenue and market presence, thereby building more profit, which is ultimately all to Sylvie's benefit."

"You mean make her a bigger target to your dad," she says, her words so scathing I'm taken aback.

I slam my hand on the desk hard enough Kat jumps in her seat. My voice is low, bitterly cold and deadly calm. "I'm not going to repeat this ever again. I had nothing to do with my dad's plot to hurt Sylvie. Had I known about it, I would have stopped it. As it stands, I turned him in to the police, thereby ensuring her safety. So, while a little fucking gratitude would be nice, I sure as hell don't expect it from the likes of you. I would, however, appreciate you leaving the caustic remarks behind because all it does is make me want to boot your ass out of here so I can get back to more important things."

Kat's eyes burn with fury but she keeps that pretty mouth shut. After a moment of continued silence, which I accept as her affirmation she understands me, I say, "I will send over the expansion plans to you. I'll even summarize the important points. You pass it on to your brother and let me know what he thinks. We can communicate by email. No sense in meeting. Will that work for you?"

"That will work fine," she clips out. "But I have a request."

I cock an eyebrow at her.

"Amend the trust agreement to remove the death clause."

I internally wince at her labeling of the paragraph that gave my father the idea to murder his granddaughter. In its simplest form, it reads that if Sylvie dies before she turns twenty-one, her winery shares revert to Mardraggon Enterprises. I'm not opposed to abolishing that from the agreement at all, but I am wondering if I can use her request to get something in return. "And why would I do that?"

"Because it's the right thing to do," she snaps.

No doubt, it's absolutely the right thing to do. But not without me getting what I desperately want. "Talk

Ethan into letting me see Sylvie and I'll gladly have it removed."

"Remove it first, then I'll talk to Ethan," she retorts.

I shake my head. "I need some good faith from your brother."

"And we would like to make sure Sylvie's protected. I think you're the one who should show good faith."

"Why? Because in case you've failed to notice, I've yet to act contrary to Sylvie's best interests."

"Maybe so, but you're a Mardraggon, and while you might not have had anything to do with your father's plot, and while you might have been the one to stop it from happening again, you're still a fucking Mardraggon and therefore cannot be trusted. You speak out of both sides of your mouth."

"Aaah," I say knowingly. "There it is. The real reason for your bluster here tonight."

"Whatever," she scoffs and leans over to pick up her purse. She rises from her chair and looks down at me. "We're done for now. Send over the information about the expansion plans. Amend the agreement. Then I'll talk to Ethan."

I don't agree to any of it, merely lock eyes with her. I'm going to do exactly what she asks for but she doesn't need to know that just now. We engage in a staring war, neither one of us blinking. I feel pettily triumphant when she looks away to glance down at her purse, reaching inside for something.

Pulling out a folded piece of paper, she offers it to me. "Sylvie wrote you a note."

I start to lunge for it but she pulls it back, out of my reach. "For once in your life, Gabe… do the right thing."

Kat drops the paper onto my desk and I resist the urge to pick it up. Instead, I keep my eyes on her as she turns on her heel and strides out of my office like she just closed a multimillion-dollar deal.

Granted, she probably won that round, but as my eyes land on the note, I can't be perturbed by it.

I unfold the paper and read the scrawling handwriting of my ten-year-old niece.

Dear Uncle Gabe,

I hope you are okay. I would like to see you but my dad says not yet. I am not mad at you and thank you for telling the police about Lionel. I hope to see you soon.

Love,
Sylvie

I blink against the sting in my eyes, reading over the simple words again. It's the best thing I could have been given right now because my main worry is how Sylvie views me. As much as my parents and I tried to turn her against the Blackburns to keep her in the fold, my father's actions have irrevocably turned her against my family. I didn't know if I would be lumped in with that generalization and it appears—for now—that I am not.

Tomorrow, I'll call my attorney and have him amend the trust agreement and then I'm going to push to see my niece.

I hear the front door open, then close. I'm left in the silence, Kat's defiance and demands lingering. I shake my head, ruminating about the one woman who always knew how to get under my skin.

Turning back to the shareholder's agreement for Mardraggon Enterprises, I try to force Kat Blackburn from my thoughts. She's a minor problem for me to handle down the road, but for now, I need to focus on taking down my father. Kat and these petty exchanges are a distraction I don't need to get embroiled in.

But the small voice inside me whispers that perhaps I want to match wits with her. Perhaps I want these confrontations. Because with every charged exchange, I'm reminded of a past I'm not sure I want to forget.

It's dangerous, this game we're playing, but I'm a Mardraggon.

Danger is our domain.

CHAPTER 5

Kat

THE DARK BARN is quiet, the gentle shuffling of the horses and the sweet scent of hay settling my frazzled nerves. That meeting with Gabe went about how I expected it to, but I thought I'd be able to walk away confident in the outcome. And while I accomplished what I'd intended—which was to establish contact and request he change the agreement—I had not expected to be so affected by the exchange.

It's utterly confusing to me how I can despise someone so thoroughly and yet feel a sliver of compassion for him. There's no doubt in my mind after talking to him that he has Sylvie's best interests at heart and that he loves her very much. I hate that it forces me to concede that Gabe actually has a heart when all evidence up until now has been to the contrary.

I make my way to Shadow's stall, using only the moonlight from the open doors I entered through to guide me. When I slide open his door and flip on his stall light, his big black head is there to greet me. I pat him on the nose, right below the white star, which is the only marking on his body. Reaching into my pocket, I pull out a peppermint for him.

Shadow's my current project horse, nearly three and a half years old and coming along nicely. He was born right here at Blackburn and Ethan gifted him to me. I took over his care immediately, spending daily time with him as a foal, touching and brushing him, sometimes leading him around on a halter to build trust. When he turned one, I began structured groundwork on a lunge line to build his muscle and stamina, as well as to introduce him to verbal commands. He learned how to wear a bit and bridle and I placed saddle pads on him so he could get used to equipment on his back. We did that for nearly a year.

Now I'm working toward breaking Shadow to be ridden. It's a slow and arduous process, sometimes taking two steps forward and one step back. For several months, he wore a saddle while I lunged him, using the time to desensitize him to the weight of the equipment and the girth holding it in place. I also used long reins on him to teach him steering and stopping commands he'll need with a rider.

Last month, I started on mounting. It's the most exciting part for me because it brings to fruition the trust we've built over the past few years. It started out with me having him stand near a mounting block and me just leaning on him. Gradually, I put more and more weight over his back until I felt confident enough to throw my leg over the saddle.

Next, I sat in the saddle and let one of the other staff lead him around at a walk while I held his reins loose. He's mastered that now without too much conniption but I never forget he's young, spirited and sometimes flighty, all while weighing close to a thousand pounds. I'm probably going to end up in the dirt a few times once I get in the saddle without any assistance, but part of all my years of training is learning how to take a fall without getting too hurt.

The main hall of lights flicker on and I turn to see Trey and Wade walking toward me.

"What are you doing here so late?" I ask. They should have been finished with their work long ago and settled into the house they share in town.

"We were going to drop off some of Miranda's lefto-ver meatloaf at your apartment but we saw your Jeep here," Wade says, holding up a paper bag.

My stomach rumbles as I give Shadow another pat and close his stall door. "Excellent. I'm starving."

Nabbing the bag from Wade, I sit down on one of the supply chests spaced periodically between the stalls, holding grooming brushes, bandages and other odds-and-ends equipment. Inside the bag sits a plastic container with a thick slice of meatloaf and mashed potatoes. Miranda even rolled up silverware in a napkin.

I plop the meal on my lap and dig in, mumbling "thanks" around my first bite. Trey and Wade are silent as they watch me, and finally I look up. "Take a picture. It lasts longer."

Trey snorts, putting a booted foot up on the chest and leaning his elbow on his thigh. "Are you going to tell us how it went with Mardraggon?"

"Oh, that." I nod as I shovel in another bite and after swallowing, I say, "It went as expected. He's a dick."

Wade laughs but Trey doesn't. "You sure you're okay dealing with him?"

I glare at my second-oldest brother. "You don't think I can because I'm a girl?"

"Girl has nothing to do with it," Trey says.

Wade steps in to defend our brother's words. "It has everything to do with us being overprotective. We'll gladly take that duty from you."

Trey nods. "You shouldn't even have to breathe the same air as that douche. We'd just like to spare you that."

The meatloaf sits like a lead ball in my stomach as I realize my brothers have no clue just how well I can handle Gabe Mardraggon. They would flip out if they had any inkling that I've had a lot of personal experience holding my own with that man.

The stadium-style lecture hall at the University of Kentucky was no less intimidating on this, my fourth day in the class over the last two weeks. The complex equations the professor wrote on the whiteboard caused my brain to fritz and I was too terrified to raise my hand for clarification because there were over two hundred other students that I was positive were a million times smarter than me. I wasn't ready for that kind of ridicule.

Instead, I sat in the very last row near the door in case I had to exit for a puking session because math literally nauseated me that much.

"Excuse me," someone said, and I tucked my legs in to let a guy move past. He ignored the open seats farther down and plopped into the one next to me.

I turned my head to offer a pathetic smile to my new seatmate, only to have my mouth drop open to see Gabe Mardraggon sitting there. I hated how handsome he was with his golden hair all mussed like he'd rolled out of bed and those eyes that glowed like pale bourbon.

I knew he'd been accepted into UK—our town is so small you know when someone farts too loud. I hadn't had the misfortune of running into him yet and figured I wouldn't since the campus was so big.

Gabe smirked and I knew him taking that seat was for no other reason than to irritate me. Our families' mutual disdain clearly drove his action, making the choice to sit next to me less innocent and more of a silent challenge.

I glared at him and turned back to my notebook. The

professor began the lecture and I took copious notes, although I understood maybe only five percent of what I was copying down. I was in the middle of tabbing a problem in my textbook when Gabe leaned over and whispered, "It's very distracting, all of this sighing you're doing."

I hadn't realized I'd been making any noises at all but that tracked. This class caused anxiety and I realized I'd been huffing and puffing it out. I spoke low through gritted teeth. "If you don't like it, move."

"Nah," he murmured, causing me to turn my gaze to him. "I like it right here."

I glanced around, looking for a nearby empty seat I could move to but there wasn't one. The class had filled up and while there were some empty seats in the row we were in, I would have to move past him to get there and he'd probably follow me. There's no doubt he was just being mean at that point.

"I take it math isn't your strong suit," he asked, again in a low rumble so that only I could hear and we wouldn't disturb the lecture.

I kept my attention on the professor but muttered, "An understatement."

"I could help you if you want."

My head whipped his way, my teeth bared in a silent snarl as I hissed softly, "Why would you even say that? I'm a Blackburn. You're a Mardraggon. We don't help each other."

"Point out the rulebook that says so," he challenged. My

mouth snapped shut because there was obviously no rulebook. Just decades upon decades of mutual loathing. His voice dropped lower. "Let's get a cup of coffee after class. I'll help you with the homework while it's still fresh from the lecture."

I was taken aback by his suggestion, the sincerity in his voice disarming. I ignored how gorgeous he was, something I'd never been able to give credence to. His muscular build and amber eyes were a devastating combination for most women, but not this Blackburn.

I was, however, able to, for just a moment, think he was something other than a Mardraggon.

Just a guy offering to help.

"Okay," I found myself saying before I could rethink it. "Coffee sounds… helpful."

"… Be careful, all right? We know the Mardraggons' true colors."

Wade's voice jolts me out of my memories and I smile at him. "Yeah… I know. I'll be careful."

The conversation shifts naturally as Trey looks out the barn door, his gaze distant. "Can't believe that bastard Lionel is out of jail already. Makes my blood boil. What I wouldn't give to serve up a little Blackburn justice."

Admittedly, I'd love to see my brothers pound Lionel to a pulp but I stop that idea in its tracks, because Wade and Trey are just stupid enough to think they could get away with some sort of retaliation. "You need to let the court system handle him. The last thing this family needs is you two to get in trouble and besides, we need to think about Sylvie first."

"Of course she's the main priority," Trey declares, his voice heavy with the gravity of the situation. "And supporting Ethan too, but at least he's got Marcie fretting over him and Sylvie. I don't think he's minding that at all."

I chuckle because seeing my big brother fall in love with Marcie has been the bright spot in all of this. Setting the container of food to the side, I ask, "How do you guys feel about Sylvie seeing Gabe? Ethan's pretty opposed to it right now."

Wade leans against the barn wall, folding his arms as he considers. "I get why Ethan's wary, but Gabe did turn in his own father. That's got to count for something, right?"

Trey shakes his head, the creases in his brow deepening. "It's not just about what Gabe did or didn't do. It's about keeping Sylvie out of any more drama. She's been through enough already."

"Yeah," I murmur, twisting the napkin between my fingers. "She mentioned wanting to see him. Gabe wants that too, but Ethan's not budging."

"Well, there's no way in hell Sylvie is going back to that house," Trey growls.

I glance up at him. "Gabe's not living there. He

bought a mansion over on Pike's Way."

"Really?" Trey says with a low whistle. "Breaking ties, I suppose."

"Maybe," I reply, although that certainly seems to be the case.

Wade kicks at a clump of dirt on the barn floor. "Sylvie's caught in the middle of all this mess. It's not fair. Maybe seeing Gabe would give her some normalcy, or at least as normal as it can get with our families."

Trey's laugh is cynical. "Normalcy? With the Mardraggons? That's a stretch."

I nod, understanding both perspectives. "It's tricky. On one hand, Sylvie deserves to have all her family around, especially the ones who care about her. I asked Gabe to amend the trust agreement to remove the reversion clause pertaining to what happens if Sylvie dies."

Snorting, Trey drops his foot from the chest. "He'll never do it. That goes against his own interests because while he might not actively want Sylvie dead, he won't give up the slight possibility if she died of some noncriminal cause, he'd get the winery."

"Perhaps," I murmur, wondering what Gabe will do. He didn't commit one way or the other and I don't know the man's mind. I thought I did at one time, but that turned out to be a lie.

"Not to change the subject," Wade says, pushing off

the wall, "but to change the subject, did you hear the old Harrison farm is up for sale? It includes all their inventory."

Trey chuckles, rubbing his chin. "Yeah, imagine us getting into the racing game. The Blackburns doing thoroughbreds. That'd shake things up."

I frown slightly, practical as ever. "But we do saddlebreds. We don't know the first thing about racing horses."

"That's not entirely true," Wade counters with a smirk. "Mom's from a thoroughbred racing family back in Ireland."

"Having a few distant cousins who breed thoroughbreds isn't exactly deep knowledge," I drawl. "Not enough to tap into the business." I seize the opportunity to lighten the mood. "Speaking of tapping into things, how's your latest conquest? Still trying to juggle three dates in one day?"

Trey's face turns a delightful shade of red as Wade bursts out laughing. Trey is a playboy and a commitment-phobe, and "dating" isn't exactly the right word for the time he spends with women.

"Hey, a man's got to have some hobbies," Trey defends himself with a sly grin.

"Keep telling yourself that," Wade says, clapping Trey on the shoulder.

I stand from the chest, placing the container of food

back in the paper bag. I intend to finish it but I'm done talking to these buffoons and it's getting late. "I'm going home. You two lock up."

"You don't get to order us around." Wade waggles his eyebrows. "We're older than you."

"In age, but not maturity," I toss back. As I walk by him, I land a solid punch on his arm and he yelps. "Besides, we both know I can kick your asses."

They howl with laughter because I can't, but they let me believe it all the same.

"Good night, sis," Wade says as he rubs his arm.

"Good night," I reply fondly, giving them a genuine smile. I love my brothers—my entire family—insanely.

And Sylvie with a fierce protectiveness I've never known.

It's why I know that I'm the best one to handle Gabe Mardraggon. Truly, I'm the only one who knows his deepest secrets and if I have to pull them out as leverage to get his compliance, I'll do it without hesitation.

Even if it means my own downfall.

CHAPTER 6

Gabe

WHILE MY MARDRAGGON ancestors settled in Shelby County, Kentucky, and opened our bourbon distillery in Shelbyville, our main offices have been in Frankfort for the last forty years. My grandfather took advantage of a good land grab as he wanted to expand our footprint and he felt it was important to be nearer to the state's capital because politics have always been soaked in the alcohol industry.

Mardraggon Enterprises takes up the top three floors of a ten-story building in the historic downtown area that was built in 1906, which has been renovated to suit my father's particular tastes.

It takes me thirty minutes to drive from my new home to the office, a place I haven't stepped foot inside of since my father's arrest. I've been working remotely, not because I'm ashamed or hiding out, but because my father has too many people loyal to him and I've been working in the shadows.

Dressed in my best bespoke suit, a fresh haircut and ten-thousand-dollar cuff links sparkling at my wrists, I enter the boardroom thirty seconds before the meeting is set to start. I purposely did this to avoid conversation. I have no desire to discuss my father, his arrest or the future of the company with most of the people here. The important conversations have already been conducted via phone or personal visits away from this building.

The Mardraggon Enterprises board of directors numbers a total of eighteen, but only twelve are needed today to carry a vote. My father, Lionel, serves as the chairman of the board, which means he's actively involved in the day-to-day management of the company and is directly accountable for the company's performance and reputation. His brother, my uncle Terrance Mardraggon, serves as the chief executive officer, a role that would normally provide insights into the company's everyday operations, challenges and strategic direction, but good old Uncle Terrance is a bit of a doormat, so my father also covers most of those functions. I'm the chief operations officer, responsible for managing the administrative and operational functions of the business, and I've served in this role for the past three years. Prior to that, I was the vice president of operations.

What do all these titles mean?

Probably not much after this meeting concludes.

My eyes immediately lock onto my father, sitting in

the largest leather chair at the end of the massive table that seats twenty-five. Terrance sits to his left and my seat is normally to his right.

Lionel looks like he's aged ten years in the two weeks since his arrest. I haven't seen him in person and only saw a glimpse of him on the nightly news when he got out of jail on bond a week ago. But that's not to say he looks frail. His jaw is set in a hard line and his eyes are glacial as they bore into me. I let my gaze slide to Terrance who quickly looks away.

Everyone in this room knows what we're doing here because I called the special meeting under the bylaws of the corporation. Everyone moves to an empty seat and I glance around at the various members—our chief financial officer, C-level executives who head up operations, marketing and human resources, and a roster of independent directors who are not part of the company's day-to-day management but rather have been chosen for their expertise in relevant fields such as finance, business strategy, law and international markets. There are other members of the board who weren't invited today, mainly because they don't have voting rights. But every one of the twelve members present will have the right to cast their choice regarding the direction of this company.

I don't take the seat next to my father but rather the one on the opposite end of the table, a massive slab of dark polished wood. I feel the weight of ancestral eyes from the portraits lining the walls, not nearly as heavy as the gazes from all the people now staring at me.

Half expecting my father to lodge an objection, I don't wait for him to take the opening. Instead, I draw first blood by giving him a polite incline of my head. "I'm glad your house arrest orders allow you to attend this meeting."

It's a stinging reminder that he's in a free fall from grace.

"This meeting is a farce," he growls.

Leaning back slightly, I interlace my fingers in front of me, maintaining my composed demeanor. "It's allowed under the bylaws," I reply coolly. "And no one provided any objection once the meeting was noticed, also required by the bylaws. You didn't even bother to object." My eyes briefly meet each board member's before settling back on my father, challenging him silently.

"I'm objecting now," he says, slamming a fist down on the table. Uncle Terrance jumps in his seat.

I glance over at Christian Radcliffe, a non-voting member of the board who is here to advise us on legalities. I lift an eyebrow and he says, "If objection is not lodged within twenty-four hours of notice, it is deemed waived."

My father mutters curses at his end of the table and I

ignore him. "As you know, I noticed this meeting of the shareholders and I'd like the record to reflect that we have twelve members here today with voting privileges, which is a proper quorum." It's absolutely astounding to me that had my dad not shown up today, there would not have been enough people to allow for a vote but I know his ego wasn't about to let him miss this. He thinks he's going to be able to control everyone here.

"I am making a motion to remove Lionel Mardraggon from his role as chairman of the board and to prevent him from having any seat on this board of directors in either a voting or non-voting capacity. My reasoning is simple… he cannot be trusted to make good decisions for this company when he's already shown to exhibit not only poor but reprehensible judgment. On top of that, our company cannot afford the damage to our reputation if we allow him to remain involved."

Clara Bennett, our company's chief financial officer and a third cousin of my father's, with her steel-gray hair impeccably coiffed, eyes me with skepticism. Michael Forbes, the youngest board member, offers a nod of support, his sleek, modern look a contrast to Clara's traditional attire. My eyes roam around the table and I note some folks look at me in support while others don't meet my eyes at all.

"I oppose this move," my father rumbles, standing from his chair and placing his hands on the table. "I am innocent until proven guilty and until such time as I'm able to show my innocence, I'm completely able to run this company. I plan on asking the court for more leniency on my house arrest so I can travel as needed. My attorneys expect that will be granted."

I glance around, spreading my hands. "Anyone else agree with this?"

Clara bristles. "Gabe, your father helped build this empire. We shouldn't dismantle his work over unproven accusations."

"It's about the company's integrity," I counter. "His alleged actions endanger everything we stand for."

Michael leans forward, his hands clasped. "The public's trust in us is at stake. Lionel's continued leadership could irreparably damage our reputation."

"But what of loyalty? Of family?" Clara retorts, her voice rising. "This is the Mardraggon legacy we're talking about!"

"The legacy doesn't excuse criminal behavior, Clara," Michael interjects firmly. "Our allegiance is to the company first."

"I'm innocent until proven guilty," my father repeats in a booming voice in a manner that's clear he means to quell the argument. The room buzzes with tension, members exchanging uneasy glances as they weigh the gravity of the decision and I start to see a triumphant glow in my father's eyes because he thinks he's in command.

But then all hell breaks loose as everyone starts arguing. No one is saying anything new or innovative, just regurgitation of what's already been laid on the table. Fingers are pointed, voices are raised and harsh, and I merely sit back in my chair and watch it all.

This goes on for almost fifteen minutes and I don't say a word. When people start to lose steam, I say, "I think everyone has had a chance to speak. I propose we vote on the removal of Lionel Mardraggon as CEO, given the severity of his charges."

I call for the vote, my heart racing. "We'll go around the room and record each vote. Aye if you're in favor of removing Lionel Mardraggon as chairman of the board. Nay if you oppose. I'll start. Aye."

I look to my right and in turn, each member declares their stance in order.

Clara's nay is adamant, but Michael's aye is equally resolved.

By the time my father is adding his own nay, it's clear we're going to have a vacant position to fill. None of this is really a surprise to me as I've been working eight of the board members sitting here today hard. I came into this meeting knowing I'd get the simple majority, but it's just icing on the cake seeing the stricken look on my father's face when Uncle Terrance adds his own aye.

The last vote is recorded and I stand from my chair. "The vote is carried. Lionel Mardraggon has been removed as chairman of the board. I'll now ask that you vacate this room immediately."

My father's icy eyes pin to me and within those depths, I can see the promise of murder. If I had any doubts about his ability to harm Sylvie, they're completely demolished now. Shoulders stiff and spine still ramrod straight, my father strides from the boardroom without a backward glance. There's a collective sigh of relief and the tension seems to dissipate.

"I'd like to make a motion to name Gabe Mardraggon as the new chairman of the board for Mardraggon Enterprises." This comes from my uncle Terrance and was not unexpected either. He and I have spoken several times over the past two weeks about this well-planned takeover event.

There's some argument—mostly from Clara—but eventually a vote carries, and I'm installed as the new chairman. We have other matters to attend to, namely filling my position as COO, and that ends up going to Michael. When the meeting concludes, Clara storms out but everyone else is at peace with the decision, even the other two who voted with my dad and Clara. We shake hands and plan another meeting tomorrow to discuss this company's future.

The room empties and I'm left alone. I walk to the windows and gaze out to the streets of downtown Frankfort, contemplating the monumental task ahead of rebuilding the legacy and the bridge between past and future. I don't have an ounce of guilt or regret doing that to my father—his betrayal to our family was far worse. The burn of fury that he tried to kill his own grand-daughter—Alaine's daughter and my niece—hasn't lessened since I found that prescription pad in his office and realized what was going on.

Pulling my phone from my inside jacket pocket, I dial my attorney. "I need an amendment to Sylvie's trust. Remove the reversion clause in its entirety."

His hesitation is palpable, even through the phone. "Gabe, are you certain? If Sylvie were to pass, the financial implications…"

Rubbing a hand at the back of my neck, I turn from the windows. "I'm aware, but Sylvie's sense of security is more important. It's about doing what's right, not what's profitable."

There's a very long beat of silence and I'm sure I've shocked him. I doubt he's ever heard a Mardraggon choose to do what was right over profit. Finally, he makes a sound of reluctance but says, "All right, Gabe. I'll prepare it."

As I end the call, the weight of my decision settles in. It's a move away from the Mardraggons' ruthless legacy.

A shift in my own personal business style.

A step toward something better for Sylvie.

Maybe for all of us.

CHAPTER 7

Kat

"**H**E'S A LITTLE antsy," Trey says, his voice flecked with worry as I stand calmly on the mounting block. My left hand holds Shadow's reins at the base of his neck, my right hand on his saddle. The big horse tosses his head and shifts his front legs.

Trey stands on the other side of him, one hand on the cheek piece of the bridle.

"He's fine," I say, and as if just to be contrary, Shadow's back end skitters away from the mounting block. I immediately let go of the reins and Trey walks him around in a wide circle twice until he's calm again.

"Maybe we should try this another day." It's both adorable and frustrating that my brother is suggesting such a thing. On one hand, I love the care and concern he has for my safety. On the other hand, I can ride just as well as he can, if not better. His worry is a little offensive.

"We're doing this today," I say with a pointed look.

"Not only is he ready, but I'm ready and I don't have a lot of time to spare. I specifically left this hour open in my schedule so I could do this."

"Fine," he grumbles and leads Shadow back over to the mounting block.

I take a moment and smooth my palm over the black horse's neck. I pull a peppermint out of my pocket, unwrap it, and offer it to him. He crunches on it with his tail flicking back and forth. He stands perfectly still so I take the reins and again place my hand on his saddle.

I decide to lean across him, something we've been practicing for weeks, but I don't go gently. I put my full weight over his back and just lie there.

Shadow doesn't so much as twitch a muscle.

"Maybe he only needed a peppermint," Trey mutters.

"Okay, let's do this." I straighten up, prepared to put my left foot in the stirrup, but I take in the slew of grooms and trainers who've come to watch. They're all standing along the wall just outside the barn office door, quietly talking as they watch me.

Not many of them can break horses to saddle so they're here to either learn something or watch me get handed my ass. My gaze starts to drop back down to the stirrup but then flies up, realizing that a man stands there in the group who is most decidedly not an employee of Blackburn Farms.

Gabe Mardraggon.

I have no clue when he came into the barn, why he's here or why he didn't announce himself. I suppose I've been so focused on getting my head in the right mental space to take this next big step that I'm not sure I would've paid him any mind had he been standing right beside Shadow.

But now that I know he's here, I'm slightly discombobulated.

I can jump off the mounting block and go see what he wants. I would do this in the privacy of the office because no doubt, we'll come to blows no matter the reason for his visit.

Or I could ignore him and keep true to the time I've carved out of my hectic schedule to conduct this very important piece of training that both my horse and I are absolutely ready for. Not only is it important, but it's one of my greatest joys as a trainer because of how complex the entire process is to get a horse to this point.

Fuck it. I'm getting on this horse.

I put my boot in the stirrup and without hesitation haul my other leg up and over Shadow's back. It comes to rest whisper light against his right side and I gain the other stirrup.

Shadow tosses his head but Trey holds him tight.

"Easy," I coo, rubbing one hand against his neck until he settles. "You've got this, big guy."

"Want me to walk you around the ring once?" Trey asks.

"No. Let go."

His green eyes tinged with concern hold mine for a second, then he reluctantly releases the bridle and takes several steps back.

Okay, buddy… let's do this.

"Walk," I say, a simple command I've been training him on but he's never had to obey with a human on his back. Elbows by my side and hands forward so I don't put any pressure on his bit, I wait to see what he does. The young horse balks for only a second before he takes a few tentative steps forward. "Walk," I repeat.

The barn is silent, all the people watching us, I'm sure holding their breath. Well, maybe not the Mardraggon. He might very well be wishing for Shadow to stomp me into the ground.

My confidence rises with every step Shadow takes and I apply slight pressure to the left rein to urge him closer to the wall. He responds beautifully, all that work with the long reins paying off.

The only goal I have is to walk him around the entire arena once and that will be enough for one day. We make it to the far end with no hiccups and I tug ever so gently on the right to get him to follow the curve of the wall. He steers beautifully but as we pass the large doors on the end, an unexpected event happens—a farm truck approaches down the gravel lot just outside the doors and while the truck's engine isn't overly loud, the crunching of rocks under the tires spooks Shadow. My first indication of his distress is the pinning of his ears backward and that's all the notice I get. My legs tighten their grip against his sides as he jumps sideways. I drop my hands, fighting against my instinct to pull hard on the reins.

"Easy," I murmur, but the truck ambles closer and the gravel crunching gets louder.

It does nothing to calm the young horse and he bucks three times before rearing up on his hind legs. I make a mad grab for his mane, still not wanting to pull on the reins, which could cause him to rear even higher. The long hair slips through my fingers and I'm holding nothing but air. I start to fall backward, which is about the worst way I could go off a horse, but at the last minute, I heave forward against gravity and throw myself to the side, kicking my boots free of the stirrups.

I vaguely hear Trey yell, "Fuck!"

A few of the trainers shout as I come free of the saddle. I'm still twisting in the air as my feet hit the ground, the momentum preventing me from sticking the landing. My body goes flying and I crash onto my left side in the dirt with a jarring thud.

The air is knocked out of me but an immediate assessment of the lack of severe pain tells me I haven't broken anything. I roll to my back, wheezing as I struggle to inhale oxygen while staring at the wooden beams of the barn's vaulted roof. I trust Trey has Shadow in hand, which is the most important thing so he doesn't hurt himself, and I just wait for my lungs to unfreeze.

My eyes widen in surprise when it's Gabe Mardraggon's face that appears first in my field of view, his expression fierce and angry. "What the fuck was that?" he snarls, before he asks, "Are you okay?"

I nod, still unable to talk but oh how I'd like to. I'd like to tell him to fuck off but I'm only at the panting stage of regaining my breath.

Gabe is physically pushed aside as Trey comes to crouch beside me, his eyes roaming my body as he takes everything in. A decided lack of tears, my inability to talk and no odd angles on my legs or arms. "Knock the breath out of you?" he asks.

I nod.

"Anything broken?"

I shake my head.

"Can you get up?"

I shrug.

Trey grins and rises, holding out his hand to me. I side lock my palm against his and when his grip is tight, I let him haul me up. The move is made much easier because to my surprise, Gabe's hand goes around my arm to help lift me from the dirt.

Trey glares at Gabe. "Get your goddamn hands off her."

"Make me," Gabe replies, his amber eyes flashing with challenge.

I pull free from both men, brushing the dirt from my clothes. My left hip is sore and as I take a few steps, I can't help the limp as I try to alleviate pressure off that side.

"You're hurt," Trey accuses.

"Sore," I whisper, still willing my lungs to fully in-flate. "I'm fine."

My head swivels, taking in Shadow as one of the grooms holds on to his bridle. He's shying back and forth and I jerk my head. "Go ahead and take him to his stall."

The man nods and leads Shadow away, who contin-ues to toss his head and prance with energy. He doesn't look scared, merely spirited right now. I watch critically to make sure I don't see any injury but he appears fine.

"I told you, you should have done this a different day," Trey grumbles as I start walking toward the office. "He's not ready."

"He's absolutely ready and I'm going to try again later tonight after I finish my work," I mutter. I'm aware that Gabe is following us, as expected. He's clearly here to talk business with me and thus, the reason I'm heading to the office rather than taking Shadow to his stall myself.

"No way you're getting back on him again," Trey says.

I stop mid-stride, turn to my brother and poke him in the chest. "Just knock it off already with the overly concerned brother routine." I poke him again hard and lift to my tiptoes to get in his face. "It's old and stupid. I'm qualified to do this job and there is no reason for me not to get right back on him. So stay out of my way."

Trey holds out his hands in surrender and I hear Gabe snort in amusement behind me. I whirl to face him, taking pleasure that his eyes flare to have my displeasure aimed at him. "And you... what are you doing here? You can't just show up without an appointment—I'm busy and my time is limited."

"Apologies, Your Highness," he replies with a mocking bow. "But I made changes to the trust agreement and I thought you might want to go over them."

My mouth falls open in surprise because I didn't think he'd do it. I'm immediately suspicious. "Exactly what changes were made?"

Gabe jerks his head toward the office. "I'll be glad to tell you in private."

"There's nothing you would tell her that I can't hear," Trey growls, stepping to place himself by my side. He crosses his arms over his chest, a resolute glare on his face.

Gabe shakes his head. "It's bad enough I have to deal with your sister but I'm not about to deal with you too." His eyes then come to me, hard and unyielding. "If you want to learn about the changes, call me and we'll set up a mutually convenient time to meet."

I'm stunned when the irritating man walks past us toward the door that leads into the small office. He makes it three long strides before I'm moved to follow. "Gabe… wait a minute."

Trey starts after us but I hold out my hand. "Stop. You're not coming."

"But—"

"No buts." I glance back and see Gabe's already walking through the door into the office, shutting it behind him. I can't assume he's waiting for me and is most likely walking right out the outer door to his car to leave.

I scramble after him but when I skid into the office, he's not walking out, rather sitting behind my desk. While I'm relieved I didn't have to chase after him, I'm pissed he's making himself at home.

"Do you mind?" I seethe, jerking my thumb. "Get out of my chair."

"Make me," he says with the corner of his mouth uplifted, eyes twinkling with challenge. That's apparently a favorite saying of his.

I roll my eyes and instead plop down on the small

75

plaid couch that's seen better days. Each Blackburn barn and arena has a small office attached to it but this is the barn I do most of my training in, so this is, for all intents and purposes, my office. The paneled walls are covered with framed photos of various shows I've competed in and strung with ribbons. Shelves are full of plaques and trophies, all of them covered in dust because who has time to keep a barn office clean when dirt floats in the air continually.

I kick my boots up on an old worn chest covered in horse magazines, holding back the wince of pain from my hip. I guarantee a bruise the size of a salad plate is forming there. I clasp my hands over my stomach and stare at Gabe, waiting for him to give me the disclosure he was so eager to reveal that he showed up without notice.

"I've removed the reversion clause from Sylvie's trust," he announces, his tone clipped as he tosses me a manila envelope and I manage to catch it before it smacks me in the face. "It already has my signature on it and only needs Ethan's."

"Why now? Decided to play the caring uncle?" I ask, unable to keep the skepticism out of my voice as I pull the papers free to examine them.

He ignores my jab. "Did you review the information I sent over about the winery? I'd like to make some decisions on investments and expansion."

"It was a lot of information." Pages upon pages that I had printed out, read once and then my eyes crossed because it was so overwhelming. I'm ashamed I have to admit, "It was difficult to make sense of it all."

"I'll be glad to sit down with you and explain it," he says neutrally, but despite the lack of any inflection, his offer dredges up an array of feelings, all of which are unpleasant.

"The way you helped me back in college?" I ask quietly. "Because wasn't that just a big setup?"

Gabe's expression hardens. "That's in the past, Kat. We're talking about the winery now."

It pisses me off he won't admit that I was nothing but a game to him. A well-thought-out, brilliantly orchestrated plan to lure me into his web so he could move in for the kill. "Hard to separate the past when it's standing right in front of me," I retort, anger bubbling up.

Gabe rises from my office chair, frustration clear in his eyes. "I'm trying to do what's right for Sylvie. No more, no less."

I can't let it go though. He wants to focus on the here and now, but it's hard to do when he caused me so much misery in the past. "I remember too well how your 'right' works, Gabe. You humiliated me when I needed you most. Which means you cannot be trusted, so how can I trust that you're wanting to do right by Sylvie?

You'll have to pardon my skepticism when you've shown to be nothing but a fraud in all you do."

He flinches, as if my words have hit their mark. Moving from around the desk, he doesn't look at me as he heads to the door. But his response shocks me. "I was a fool back then, Kat. But I'm not that person anymore. And it was never a setup. Never!"

"You say that, but it's hard to tell which Gabe Mardraggon I'm dealing with—the bully or the businessman," I say, standing my ground.

Turning to face me, Gabe clenches his jaw, his eyes darkening. "I'm always the businessman but in this instance, I'm just Sylvie's uncle trying to secure her legacy because that's what my sister wanted."

Admittedly, those words sound genuine and I suppose the ease by which he granted my request to change the agreement to Sylvie's benefit and his detriment speaks even louder. For a moment, there's a flicker of something else in his eyes—regret, maybe? But it's gone as quickly as it appeared.

"I'll email you some dates I have open if you want to sit down and go over the winery stuff together so I can explain it." Gabe reaches for the door, but his eyes pin me with an unyielding intensity. "Have Ethan sign the trust agreement and get it back to me to file. Then I want to see Sylvie."

There's no doubt he deserves it at this point and I

know it's something Sylvie wants. "I'll arrange it."

Gabe turns and strides out, leaving me with a whirlwind of papers and mixed emotions. I flip through the trust agreement, seeing his scrawling signature on the last page. Dealing with him is going to be more challenging than I thought, both professionally and personally.

Glancing at my watch, I see I have plenty of time to take this over to Ethan, especially since my ride with Shadow got shortened. I push up from the couch, not holding back the groan of pain from my hip. I brush it aside though, still intent on getting back up on the gelding tonight.

I nab my phone from the desk and send Ethan a text. *Where are you?*

Main house, he replies.

My fingers tap out a short response. *On my way to see you.*

It takes me no more than five minutes to traverse the path from the training barn up to the house in my utility vehicle. I see Marcie's car in the driveway and smile. I've been so busy this last week trying to keep up with my regular work plus the additional duties I've taken off Ethan, I've hardly been to the main house. I think Marcie's staying over now at night, which is a good thing as that's just extra support for Sylvie. Say what you will about my brother and Marcie falling in love, but the flame-haired school principal has become a mother to Sylvie in all ways. I expect Ethan and Marcie will marry sooner rather than later and I'm here for it.

After removing my boots in the mudroom, I enter through the kitchen. It's Miranda's day off, so there's no delicious smell of simmering dinner or baking sweets. I do find Marcie and Sylvie at the kitchen nook table, bent over a workbook together.

Their heads raise and both smile at me before Marcie stands up. We move toward each other, a hug first on our agenda.

"Long time no see, stranger," I say as I bend to wrap her small frame in an embrace.

"You're working too hard," she murmurs, squeezing me tight. She then lowers her voice so only I can hear. "Thank you for helping Ethan. You and your brothers really stepped up and it's made all the difference."

"Glad to," I assure her and after we pull apart, I ruffle Sylvie's hair. "What's up, munchkin?"

She hoists her book. "Fractions."

I wrinkle my nose. I still hate math. "Gross."

"So easy," she counters in her lilting French accent.

"Oh yeah," I tease, grabbing the book to look at her work. "If it's so easy, why is Marcie helping you?"

Marcie laughs as I look at Sylvie's answers, her handwriting absolutely perfect. "Not helping her. Checking her work."

I toss the book back down. "Glad you're doing that because I draw the line at math."

Sylvie giggles, sliding the workbook closer to her. Marcie's hand comes to my arm. "Ethan's finishing up a few things in his office, but we're going out for Italian after he's done. Want to join us?"

"I'd love to but I've got a date with a handsome boy later tonight," I reply, my grin broadening into a playful smirk.

Marcie's eyes flare wide and she dips her head in close. "Oh, really. Do tell?"

"He's tall, muscular, dark and handsome." Marcie's eyes twinkle with interest. I hold my hand up above my head. "He's about seventeen hands tall and has the maturity of a toddler."

She rolls her eyes. "A freaking horse? Why can't you be normal and date so I have interesting gossip to discuss with Ethan?"

"Who has time to date?" I ask, walking backward toward the hallway that leads to Ethan's office. "Besides... I much prefer horses."

Marcie waves me off, shaking her head. I start to turn away but Sylvie stops me. "Aunt Kat, have you talked to Uncle Gabe lately?"

I'm not ready to tell her about our meeting today because Ethan needs to hear those details first, but I nod at her. "Saw him just a little bit ago and I'm on my way to discuss some things with your dad now."

Sylvie's eyes alight with hope but thankfully she

doesn't press me on seeing Gabe right now. It's not my decision to make, but I'll push Ethan to allow it to happen.

I find Ethan bent over his desk, consternation on his face. His head pops up when I walk in and he rubs at his eyes before yawning. "Hey."

"Hey," I say as I settle into a chair. I toss the envelope on his desk and nod at it. "Gabe amended the trust agreement, removing the reversion clause. All you need to do is sign it and that winery will never go back to the Mardraggons."

Ethan's dark eyebrows rise. "Seriously?"

"Seriously," I confirm with a nod.

"I didn't think he'd ever do that."

I shrug. I had my doubts, but part of me could see Gabe doing what was in Sylvie's best interests. "Means that winery will stay within the Blackburn family."

"Guess we better really learn the business now, huh?" Ethan muses, settling back in his chair.

"Why not? Trey and Wade think we should get into breeding thoroughbreds."

Ethan groans as he shakes his head. "I don't need one more thing on our plate right now."

"We just stay the course with everything," I say, injecting a note of firm assurance into my voice. "There are apparently some decisions that need to be made about the winery. Gabe and I are going to set up a meeting to go over everything."

"You don't sound too bent out of shape about it," Ethan muses, his eyes studying me critically.

"It's a necessary evil," I reply, blowing off his keen perception. I have to admit, Gabe amending that trust agreement has gone a long way toward soothing some of the disdain I have for the man.

Not all of it though.

Ethan looks out the window, the sun setting over the rolling pastures. "Gabe sure is making some bold statements when it comes to family loyalty."

"What do you mean? He's done something else other than amend the trust?"

Gaze coming back to me, Ethan nods with a half smile. "It hasn't been in the news, but I heard through the grapevine that Gabe had Lionel removed as chairman of the board of Mardraggon Enterprises. Apparently staged a very successful coup and had himself named the new chairman."

"Oh, wow," I murmur in amazement. That indeed makes a very loud statement about his loyalties to his father.

Then again, I could argue the only reason he amend-ed that trust was to see Sylvie so he could have a direct influence over her. Gabe has only ever been loyal to himself.

Unbidden and most certainly unwanted, a flashback

hits me hard of a time when I didn't think that about Gabe.

A cool fall day in Lexington, Gabe and I were studying together. The sun was bright and we both wore UK sweatshirts, the outdoor temps comfortable enough to spread out on a blanket. He'd been helping me with math the last few weeks and I'd found a surprising comfort in his presence.

Gabe had his nose buried in a textbook for his economics class and I was lying on my stomach, diligently working through complex equations that were admittedly a bit easier to digest with Gabe's easy style of teaching.

I was comfortable in the silence with him and ignored the other students walking by as I concentrated on the work. It was a difficult problem and I tapped my pencil's eraser against my chin while I contemplated. I was determined to figure it out on my own and not ask Gabe to guide me through it. I'd rather rely on him to check my answers.

My entire body locked tight when Gabe reached out and moved a lock of my hair back behind my ear. It was the first time he'd ever touched me and I looked at him in surprise.

His golden eyes shone bright in the sun and we just stared at each other a long moment. Finally, I had to ask. "Why did you do that?"

"Been wanting to do that for a long time," he replied.

It was such a tender moment of touch, soft words laced with yearning. A stark contrast to the animosity of our families and the natural rift that stretched between us.

It was utterly confusing because Gabe never came across

as anything other than a new friend who was willing to help me with my schoolwork.

"Can I take you out to dinner tonight?" he asked.

"As in a date?" My mouth gaped. "You can't be serious."

He waved an impatient hand. "Of course I can be serious."

"Our families hate each other. We hate…" My words trailed off as I realized… I didn't hate him the way I'd been taught to. Something had changed in the last few weeks, and he no longer seemed like an enemy. "Our parents won't approve."

"They don't have to know," he replied, and there was something very appealing about having a secret like this. It was exciting, being away at college in this new little bubble of freedom and experiencing new opportunities.

Gabe Mardraggon was forbidden and God help me, it made him sexier.

My answer sealed our fate. "Okay… I'll go out to dinner with you."

"Want to come out to dinner with us tonight?" Ethan's voice busts through my memories. He's staring down at the trust agreement which is lucky for me, as my cheeks feel heated.

"Um, no. Thanks. I'm working on Shadow this evening." I stand from the chair, move to the edge of the desk and put my hand over the trust agreement so Ethan is forced to look up at me. "I think Gabe has earned the right to see Sylvie."

That suggestion troubles my brother, as I expected it would. He shakes his head ruefully. "I don't know, Kat."

"Sylvie wants it," I point out. "Your daughter wants this relationship."

Ethan scrubs his hands over his face, his expression miserable as he sighs. "Fine. I'll set something up with him."

"I'll be glad to chaperone if you want me to. I'm already dealing with him on the winery."

"Would you really?" Ethan asks, his expression lighting up with a surge of relief. "I just don't have it in me to be around anyone in that family. Logically, I understand he's not his father, but all I see is a Mardraggon and it makes me furious what they did."

"I understand," I say, moving my hand over to lay on top of his. "I got this, Ethan."

CHAPTER 8

Gabe

PACING BACK AND forth in my home office, I rub at my neck, which has tightened into knots. "Clara… I do not have time to rehash all of this with you. My father is no longer chairman. The vote was properly called for and executed. You need to deal with it or you can resign your position. Which is it going to be?"

"I am going to hold you accountable," she snaps with the iron bite of a woman who's been helping to helm the empire for decades. "You may think you know what you're doing, but you're just a young pup and you are out of your league."

Someone with a lesser ego might be intimidated by her rebuke, but I recognize what this is. Clara is fearful she'll be ousted right alongside my father. She represents part of the old guard. She sees that I want to bring new and young blood onto the board because I have a greater vision than my father did.

Simply put, she's concerned for her livelihood.

"Clara, you are a vital and integral part of this organization. I need people like you and Uncle Terrance on the board who can help advise me and who are willing to let me guide this ship under such advice. But I can't battle you and do my job at the same time. You need to decide which way it's going to be."

I listen to her ramble for another five minutes, but I note that she's no longer playing the blame game for what I did to my father. Deep down she knows we cannot have an accused attempted murderer on our board. It would kill our reputation and our product.

Ultimately, we end the call with the promise to meet tomorrow for lunch so we can discuss her concerns. I'm confident I can get her reined in but to be on the safe side, I shoot a quick text to Uncle Terrance and invite him to join us. He's an ally no one expected me to have since he's incredibly close to my father and has essentially been his right-hand man. I know it was a dagger to Lionel's heart when Uncle Terrance voted against him, but my uncle saw the writing on the wall and he knew it was time to jump ship.

After pocketing my phone, I move to my desk and stuff several folders in my briefcase. I glance around my new home office, loving the casual comfort. I love even more not having to wear a suit when I choose to work from here rather than the office and while my jeans and shirt are designer, they're still representative of some of the changes happening with me.

As awesome as it was to kick my dad off the board of directors, the real victory was in getting Ethan's agreement to let me see Sylvie. I dropped the revised trust agreement off yesterday with Kat and before I went to bed last night, she told me via text that Ethan agreed. He wasn't about to let me get my hands on her alone and I understand that. It appears that Kat is to be our chaperone, so I'm headed to Blackburn Farms now to spend the afternoon with my niece.

I sling the briefcase over my shoulder and move to the couch to grab the two shopping bags filled with presents for Sylvie. I feel no need to buy her affection as I'm confident in the bond I've developed with her since the day she was born, but it makes me feel good to give her something to bring a smile to her face. God knows she needs it.

Sylvie and I have always been tight. I went to France a handful of times each year to visit and we stayed in frequent contact by phone or FaceTime. That was a reflection of the rock-solid bond I had with my sister Alaine, born of being raised in the same cold sterile home environment. We really only had each other.

When Alaine got sick with brain cancer and we realized she was dying, my bond with Sylvie strengthened even more. Alaine and Sylvie came to live with us in Kentucky and when Sylvie wasn't spending time with her mother, she was at my side.

I had even fancied in my mind that I would be the one to raise Sylvie after my sister died. It made the most sense and I even started making plans to get out from under my parents' roof and buy a home Sylvie and I could live in.

That all went to hell after the truth came out that Ethan Blackburn was Sylvie's father. The cruel twist of betrayal from my sister was that she wanted Sylvie to live with him and not me.

Naturally, I banded with my parents to make sure that didn't happen. Sylvie is a Mardraggon, not a Blackburn. I aligned with my parents' efforts to do everything we could to turn Sylvie against Ethan. For me, it wasn't about the winery. I didn't care at all what happened to it because I was more focused on our bourbon empire, which is the real moneymaker.

But as a Mardraggon, I hated the Blackburns. The long-standing divide would never be bridged and I would keep Sylvie on our side.

While my father was apparently plotting the murder of his granddaughter, I just wanted to keep her bonded to me. I could not stomach the thought of Sylvie becoming a Blackburn nor could I envision her spending any time with them. If she developed ties to that family that meant I would have to deal with them, and I didn't want them in my life.

Most of all, I did not want Kat there. In truth, that was a huge driving factor in my zeal to keep Sylvie separated from the Blackburns. I could not foresee a life where our families barbecued together because one precocious child closed the gap. That was a dream I once had a long time ago, but it died. It was mostly my fault when it crashed and burned, and I never planned to put myself into that position again.

But I'm in the thick of it now.

Sylvie is a Blackburn, and she has nothing of the Mardraggons in her other than her mother's DNA. She is nothing like her grandparents and I see very little of me within her because I can be ruthless in pursuit of what I want. But now I have to play nice because I hold no leverage with Ethan Blackburn and if I want Sylvie in my life, that means I have to accept the Blackburns to some extent. Frustrating beyond measure, that means Kat is back in my life now too.

She is the biggest complicating factor I face. She is what's causing me the most stress right now because no matter how snide our exchanges are or how deep our bitter feelings run, I am still drawn to the woman.

I still want her.

And apparently, I still care for her because when she fell off that horse yesterday, my heart stopped cold in my chest. The fall was brutal and I was afraid she was dead. I took off running across the barn without thought as to how it might look. Luckily, Kat was knocked too silly to understand the meaning behind my actions and Trey was too conceited in the hatred between us all that he didn't even pay attention.

It was a potent reminder that Kat Blackburn still has power over me and if I allow myself to succumb to it, I'll slide down an incredibly slippery slope. I know this because it happened once before. We were young, dumb and foolish, but we were crazy about each other.

I rapped my knuckles softly on the door to Kat's dorm room, looking left and right to make sure nobody saw me. It was close to midnight and her roommate was staying over at her boyfriend's house. While this was a coed dorm, I could've gotten in serious trouble for being on the female floor at this time of night. But this wasn't the first time I'd been here nor would it be my last. Nothing would keep me away from Kat.

She swung open the door and before I could even level a smile her way, her hands gripped my T-shirt and she dragged me inside. I'm not sure who closed the door, but all that mattered was that her mouth was on mine and my hands were on her. We fumbled our way through hot kisses and tearing off each other's clothes. We fell onto her bed and I whispered dirty things in her ear.

Our tutoring relationship didn't last long. An impromptu casual dinner turned into a few beers turned into a few kisses and that turned into a firestorm between us. Kat and I always burned hot together, a relationship born from hate but then evolved through secrecy. It was complicated and exciting and I always felt like I was drowning in her presence. I sunk into her body that night, feeling more at home than I ever had anywhere in my life. And after we both found the height of pleasure in her narrow bed, we lay naked in each other's arms, talking about the future.

Christmas was coming up and both of us were going home for nearly three weeks. We had no clue what that would look like because no one knew we were seeing each other. Sequestered away at the University of Kentucky and being careful not to be seen in public, since I had other family members and friends enrolled, we kept the truth hidden.

"We can meet up in the empty apartment above the tack room," Kat suggested as her fingers trailed over my chest.

"I can always get a hotel room. We could go spend a weekend in Louisville."

Kat sighed contentedly. "That sounds nice. But I wish we didn't have to sneak around."

"I wish that too, but it's not an option to tell our families right now. We're going to have to figure a way to ease into it."

"I know," she said dejectedly. "It's just so stupid that something that happened eons ago should affect us. The original feud has nothing to do with you and me."

She wasn't wrong about that. It all began in the mid-1850s, a tale of tragic love and betrayal. Elizabeth Blackburn and Henry Mardraggon, our ancestors, were set to unite our families through marriage. But fate, laced with malice, intervened. Vicious rumors about Elizabeth emerged, as poisonous as nightshade, and the patriarchs of both families—driven by pride more than reason—drew their pistols in a heated argument. A shot fired, a life lost. Henry Mardraggon lay dead, and with him, the hope of unity.

The grief was too much for Elizabeth Blackburn. She took her own life weeks later, leaving behind a legacy of heartache and anger. The Blackburns blamed the Mardraggons, the Mardraggons blamed the Blackburns, and just like that, a feud was born, growing stronger with each subsequent generation.

And we're still paying for all that heartache.

"It's not just the original feud," I pointed out. "It's our families continually hurting one another. Hell, my father beat your dad on a land purchase not but eight years ago."

I hold my breath waiting to see if the reminder of that unpleasant incident will enrage Kat because my dad was unscrupulous in using government favors to practically steal the land from Tommy Blackburn. The Mardraggons didn't need it but we didn't want the Blackburns to have it. We've never really talked about all the terrible things our families have done to each other, but this one deepened the hatred in these modern times.

I'm so relieved when she says, "I still say that has nothing to do with us."

But I'm also a realist and I had to point out, "Doesn't

it? I'm going to be head of Mardraggon Enterprises one day and we'll always have that land that your family needed to expand the farm."

Kat lifted her head and grinned down at me. "You could give it back."

I lifted my own head and kissed her before saying, "You could buy it from me."

I meant it in jest since she's the one who started the teasing, but her face crumbled. "This is why we can't work."

I took her jaw in my hand. "Don't say that. We'll find a way."

And I kissed her again and rolled her back under me and we forgot all about the things that can tear us apart and concentrated on what we had together.

The chimes of my doorbell brings me back to the present and I set my briefcase down next to the shopping bags. I check my watch as I head to the front door, wondering who it might be. Very few people know I live here now, and I haven't ordered anything to be delivered.

I open the door and find two men standing on the porch, their hands clasped in front of them. They're wearing expensive suits but they look decidedly un-businesslike. Both tall and beefy, one has blond hair slicked back and the other has dark hair in a short crew cut. The blond smiles at me genially, the dark-haired one scowls, and I spy a line of tattoos creeping up past the collar of his dress shirt.

"Can I help you?" I ask, my gaze cutting back and forth between them.

"My name's Kravitz," the blond says, reaching out to hand me a business card. He then throws a thumb toward his tattooed partner. "That's Bellamy."

"Just Kravitz? Just Bellamy? Is that sort of like Madonna or P!nk?" I glance down at the card and see the name Clinton Rafferty. There's an address and phone number, but I lift my gaze back up to the man who handed it to me.

Kravitz is amused by my questions but Bellamy scowls. "We work for Mr. Rafferty and we would like a minute of your time."

I have no fucking clue what this is about but I was on my way out the door for what promises to be a pleasant afternoon. "I'm sorry, but I've got an appointment to get to. If you would like to tell me what this is about, we could set another time to meet."

Kravitz inclines his head. "This won't take long, Mr. Mardraggon. We're here about a matter involving your father."

"Then I suggest you go see my father," I say, warning tingles running up my spine, his tone clearly threatening.

"Your father can't help us. We understand he's been ousted from Mardraggon Enterprises and that you're in charge now."

I don't respond but merely stare at the man.

"Your father owes Mr. Rafferty a case of the Mardraggon 1921 Shadow Reserve Barrel. We're here to collect it."

My eyes widen in shock and I can't help but laugh. "You've got to be kidding me."

"Your father bet that case in a high-stakes poker game with Mr. Rafferty. Your father lost and has yet to pay the debt. Mr. Rafferty believes you are the best person to deliver. You have one week to hand it over."

"You're fucking crazy," I growl at the men, my eyes cutting between the two. "My father isn't a gambler. He doesn't believe in wasting hard-earned money."

I'm stunned when Bellamy says, "Your father had a severe addiction to horse gambling and later found a love of poker, although he was quite bad at it. We have a marker for the case of bourbon."

"That's a shame then because my father doesn't own the bourbon you're talking about therefore he couldn't have given you a marker. It belongs to the company."

Kravitz nods as if he understands but his smile is chilling. "It's a good thing you're the new chairman of the board then. Like I said, you're the best person to ensure it gets delivered in satisfaction of the debt."

"I'm sorry you came all this way, gentlemen. I have no intention of turning the case over to you." The Mardraggon 1921 Shadow Reserve Barrel was a single case of high-quality, rare bourbon that our distillery produced in 1921. Bourbon doesn't age or change once it's bottled, unlike wine, so its shelf life when unopened can be quite long. The key factors for maintaining its quality over years or even decades are proper storage conditions, away from direct sunlight and at a stable, moderate temperature. Therefore, an unopened bottle of bourbon, especially if it's a rare or vintage variety, can remain good to drink for many years.

Only twelve bottles were made and expertly stored. The case itself is valued at over two million dollars. It's not something that would ever be sold nor would it be gambled away in a poker game as it is a physical representation of our family's legacy. "I would like you both to leave my property and not come back again."

Neither man seems offended and Kravitz is blasé when he says, "You have one week. We'll be back."

They turn to walk toward a dark Suburban with tinted windows parked on the other side of the circular driveway and I feel compelled to make myself clear. "You can come back, but there won't be any bourbon here for you."

Bellamy turns, his eyes sparkling with the promise of violence. "If the bourbon isn't here, there's going to be pain. We'll start with your father."

They could beat the shit out of my father for all I care. I don't say that though. I don't say anything because it's clear these two men don't have any authority to negotiate or stop whatever train my dad has set into motion by his poor choices. I most certainly have no authority to produce the case of bourbon they claim is held by a marker, nor would I want to if I had the ability. Mr. Rafferty is shit out of luck, but my dad has enough money I'm sure he can cover the cost of the marker, regardless of how bad his gambling debts are.

I don't respond and patiently wait for the men to leave, the Suburban disappearing down the long driveway. I walk back into the house to gather my briefcase and Sylvie's presents. The excitement of seeing my niece has me forgetting all about the unpleasantness of that visit.

I don't even try to analyze that a part of me is excited to see Kat as well.

CHAPTER 9

Kat

LOOKING AROUND MY small apartment, I wonder what memories this will evoke for Gabe today. It was so different when we were using it to sneak around back in college during the summer months, all bare bones living for transient employees. Now it screams Kat Blackburn with all my redecorating, but I'm not sure Gabe really knows who Kat Blackburn is anymore.

We agreed to let Gabe and Sylvie have time here today rather than at the big house. While the police have let our family know that their investigation into both Gabe and Rosemund has confirmed that Lionel acted alone, Ethan is still tense about anything dealing with the Mardraggons and it's best to keep the men separated. Ideally, we'd spend some time outdoors because the end of May in Kentucky is beautiful, but it's been raining steadily all day.

So it's going to be me, Gabe and Sylvie in my little seven-hundred-square-foot apartment that holds the ghosts of memories of my time with Gabe.

For over a year, we kept our relationship secret and met up here on school breaks and summer vacations. It's above one of the smaller tack rooms out near the retirement pastures and can't be seen from the main house. It became a special place for us because the more time we spent together, the harder we fell for each other. It wasn't all the time but it was enough that I can see Gabe in nearly every corner of this place.

Sylvie is at my small kitchen table that only seats two, finishing up her homework. I watch as her pencil flies across her math problems, her brow furrowed in concentration. I'm surprised she can focus because she's been nearly beside herself with excitement that her uncle is coming over.

It nearly broke my heart when she said, "Gabe is proof the Mardraggons have good in them."

She really needs to believe that. The betrayal of Lionel in attempting to kill her, and the further betrayal of Rosemund who has stuck by his side, rattled my niece something fierce. But Gabe loves her, has shown he will protect her, and this is evidence to Sylvie that the last connection she has to her mom is a trusted family member.

Personally, I wouldn't trust him as far as I can throw him, but that's not for me to say to Sylvie. At this point, no one wants to give her doubts and she needs security in the knowledge that we all love her. That includes Gabe.

The sound of a vehicle coming up the gravel lane approaches and Sylvie's head pops up. "He's here."

Yes he is, and my heart thunders within my chest. There was a time when Gabe could just look at me and I'd feel faint from the thrill of it. Now my traitorous heartbeat has more to do with the confusing circumstances I find myself in, having to deal with a man I once cared a great deal for and then had more reason to hate him than any long-standing feud could deliver.

The reason it's complicated is because even though we snipe at each other, I saw something in Gabe yesterday that I thought I'd never see again.

Care.

Lying in the dirt, the breath knocked out of me from my fall off Shadow, Gabe came into view and I saw genuine, deep-rooted fear etched on his beautiful face. Not just concern for another human being, but terror for my well-being, and it told me that while things ended very badly between us, Gabe still cares about me.

I've been trying to wrap my head around that fact all day and now I'm about to come face-to-face with the man who is plaguing my thoughts both day and night.

A wooden staircase leads up to my apartment door and we can hear Gabe running up it, most likely to avoid the steady fall of rain. Sylvie is there to greet him and I hate that he looks so damn good as he steps in after shaking off his umbrella.

I truly never gave Gabe Mardraggon much of a second look during childhood and our adolescent years. Our families would run into one another at various occasions, my brothers played football and baseball against him, and Shelbyville is so small, we'd sometimes have occasion to meet on the streets. It wasn't until Gabe sat beside me that day in math class and offered to tutor me that I let myself see past the ingrained hate.

Allowed myself to appreciate how tall and muscular he was. The way his dark gold hair and molten amber eyes seemed brilliantly kissed by the sun and made him appear godlike. The way other women tried to catch his attention and other men tried to emulate him. Yes, he had gobs of money and dressed in the best clothes and drove the fanciest cars, but it was the way he listened to me that really had me looking at him differently. Our tutoring sessions were legit and he helped me tremendously, but we spent a lot of time talking about things other than math.

I got to know who I thought was the real Gabe Mardraggon and God help me, I was attracted to every inch of him. It wasn't long before I cared so deeply for him, I couldn't imagine a life without him by my side.

Even now, dressed in a polo shirt and dark jeans, he exudes wealth, confidence and sex appeal. His eyes briefly land on me but the stare is broken when Sylvie flings herself into his arms with enough force he stumbles back, a laugh rumbling from him.

I wince, hearing that sound. Unrestrained and joyful, deep and resonant, it fills the room with its warmth. It's genuine and a potent reminder there's a real man under the veneer of wealth and selfishness.

"Uncle Gabe," Sylvie gushes, pulling him inside by the hand. "I'm so glad you came over."

She hugs him again and it's then that I notice he's holding several bags in one hand and can't really reciprocate. I lunge forward, grabbing the bags from him as he lets his briefcase slide off his shoulder. "Here… let me take those."

Gabe doesn't look at me but the way his eyes light up when he's able to wrap his niece in a hug tells me she's extremely important to him. She's not a means to a winery and he's not acting out of intense guilt. He loves her. It's that simple.

"I brought you some presents," Gabe says, and Sylvie pulls back, her eyes sparkling. He nods at the bags in my hand but says, "First, catch me up on how school has been."

I'm stunned as the two talk, Sylvie having led him over to the couch. I set the bags down on the floor next to them and move into the kitchen to start prepping dinner. Sylvie is going back to the main house to eat with the family but Gabe is staying here to give me a winery

101 lesson. I hadn't invited him for dinner nor does he have expectations I'll feed him, but I'm hungry after a long day of working and have more work to do with Gabe after Sylvie leaves. I intend to eat so it's just as easy to make enough for two.

I listen intently as Gabe asks Sylvie thoughtful questions about her understanding of math concepts, how her opinion writing is progressing—not even sure what that means—and even discusses world events that he's clearly taught her about in the past. The conversation doesn't lag and I can see that Sylvie is not only completely comfortable in his presence, she respects him. More than anything, I note that Gabe provides something for her none of us Blackburns can.

Within the ease of Sylvie's smile and her obvious connection on a familial level, Gabe is healing the wounds that Lionel wrought. He's validating to his niece that there is good in the Mardraggon blood and conversely, there is nothing bad in her.

Tears prick my eyes at the revelation and I don't even try to dismiss it as bogus. My brothers, my sister and my parents all have their misgivings about Gabriel Mardraggon but they don't know that I've observed the goodness in him before.

Just as I know inside lurks the potential for harm.

The difference between my experience and Sylvie's, however, lies in the fact that he loves her probably more than anything in this world. No matter what Gabe and I had, it was never real love, as proven by how easily he abandoned the ideals we were striving for.

As I put together a cold grilled chicken salad, I continue to listen to the interplay between uncle and niece. My ears tune sharp though, when Sylvie says, "I have something important to ask you and I'm nervous about it."

My hands still on the strips of chicken I'm dicing, my head turning slightly their way. Gabe is on one end of the couch facing her, his arm draped casually over the back. Sylvie is on the middle cushion, head bowed and black hair hiding her face.

"You can tell me anything, squirt. You know that." Though his words are light and encouraging, I see the distress in his eyes. It clears when she lifts her gaze to him and he smiles at her.

"My birth certificate has Mardraggon as my last name. Originally, it didn't list my dad as my father. Now it's been added, but my last name has stayed the same." Her words trail off and I see where she's going with this.

Gabe does too and his smile softens with understanding. "You want to change your last name to Blackburn."

She nods, head ducking again and voice small. "I talked to my dad about it and he said that would not be a problem, but I wanted to let you know." She takes a deep breath, perhaps garnering courage, and lifts her eyes back to the one person who might be hurt over this. "I don't want you to be mad at me."

Hand lifting from the back of the couch, Gabe tugs playfully on Sylvie's hair in an attempt to lighten things. "Why would I be mad at you?"

"Because…" She fumbles for the right words but gets them out in a mad rush, indicating to me that she's been practicing. "Because I don't want you to think I'm trying to erase my mom by giving up her last name."

"Oh, honey," Gabe murmurs, his hand going to her shoulder for a gentle squeeze. "You couldn't erase your mother if you tried. I see so much of her in you and that will never change. Mardraggon is just a last name, but I do understand that it's a name that will never inspire pride or represent love to you, and for that, I'm sorry."

Sylvie shakes her head. "You shouldn't be sorry."

"I'm sorry it's making you feel bad about yourself and I think it's a brilliant idea for you to change your last name to Blackburn. Your mother wanted you to be with Ethan, and I have to believe that means she'd want you to share his last name too."

Sylvie's eyes round with pure desire to believe those words. "Really?"

"Really," he assures her. "You get your father working on that as fast as possible, okay?"

My conflicted feelings make my stomach roll. How easy it is for Gabe to grant respect to Sylvie, Ethan and the Blackburn name. Gone is the ire for our family and the shame in having a connection to it. He gives it so willingly to Sylvie and yet denied it all to me.

I'm not selfish enough to try to refute that this is an apples-and-oranges situation. He and I were barely nineteen, trying to navigate this ages-old feud between our families. Now Gabe is older, more mature.

Sylvie is also his blood, the closest tie he has to his beloved sister. He'd gladly give his niece the world. I wasn't even quite his girlfriend. More of an infatuation if I had to put a label on what we had.

At least, that's how I felt in the end. The same old arguments took up the precious moments we had to steal to be together.

"Gabe, we can't keep hiding. Let's tell our families." That was my mantra. My most fervent wish.

His was radically different. *"Kat, you know we can't. It'll be a disaster. Do you think our families will just accept this? It'll reignite everything."*

Over and over again, the same old words. The same wishes and denials. And yet, I couldn't walk away from him. My heart was involved and I was sure, deep down, his was right along with me. That when it truly mattered, Gabe would be brave enough to step under the microscope of our families' scrutiny and we'd both force them to accept that the feud was ending with us.

It didn't work out that way and even after eight years

apart and plenty of moving on, I'm still as bitter and resentful as I was back then.

I was making my way across the quad, the crisp autumn air of my sophomore year filled with the chatter and laughter of students back from fall break. While Gabe and I managed to see each other a few times, now that we were back on campus, we could be freer to be the couple we clearly had become. We still stayed in the shadows but the acreage was greater here in Lexington than it was back home in Shelbyville.

I was on my way to meet Gabe at his off-campus house. His roommate was away for the weekend and we had unfettered time to ourselves. I was running a little early but Gabe had given me a key to his place, surely a sign that he was ready to commit even deeper to me. I smiled as I crossed an intersection, only a few blocks from his house. Maybe I'd strip down naked and just wait in bed for him.

The one thing Gabe excelled at was getting me to release my inner sex goddess. I never knew physical intimacy could be so profound and yet liberating at the same time. He made me feel beautiful, no more so than when he was worshipping me in bed.

My head was in the stars when I reached his house so I didn't really see Derek Mardraggon until I almost ran into him. He was coming down the porch steps, his cell phone pressed to his ear as he was talking to someone.

Derek was Gabe's first cousin, second son to Terrance Mardraggon. He and Gabe weren't overly close, but Derek was a freshman and Gabe had been helping him navigate first-year life at the University of Kentucky. I was so shocked to see him, and him me, that we came to a stop and just stared at each other.

My heart pounded as I realized this did not look good, me waltzing up to Gabe's place as if I belonged there. While I wanted nothing more than for me and Gabe to tell the family, I knew that this was not the way to do it. Mind buzzing with potential excuses as to why I was here, it hit me that I was merely walking down the block. I wasn't necessarily headed to Gabe's place as far as Derek knew.

With that in mind, I continued walking down the sidewalk, intending to make a wide berth around where Derek stood at the bottom of Gabe's steps. My eyes were on the ground, my shoulders hunched as I held tight to the pack on my back, hoping it would look like nothing more than a Blackburn wanting to avoid confrontation with a Mardraggon.

No such luck though, as Derek stepped into my path, bringing me up short. He wasn't overly big, standing only a few inches taller than my five-seven height. But as I looked up at him, the smug superiority on his face made me feel about three inches tall.

"I knew I smelled something foul on the wind," he said as his eyes ran up and down me in disgust.

I had to bite my tongue not to hurl back an insult. "I don't have time for childish assholes."

I tried to step around Derek but he moved quickly,

blocking my exit. "Oh, don't play so coy with me, Kat. I mean… you're a Blackburn and all, but I could make an exception if you wanted to see what a real man was like."

I almost gagged when he reached out and brushed hair back from my face. Once again, eyes ran down my body and this time, they weren't mocking and cruel but held lewd intentions within their muddy brown depths.

His fingers trailed along my neck and the touch was so abhorrent that I scrambled away from him, coming up against a large oak tree in the corner of Gabe's yard.

Derek was fast, moving to cage me in against the tree with one palm on the rough bark and the other tugging on a lock of my hair. "What do you say we go back to my place? It will be a step up for you and I've never been too proud to slum it."

Enraged, my hands flew to his chest and I shoved him hard. "You're a pig."

"Hey," I heard Gabe call out and my head turned to see him walking down the sidewalk, his eyes flicking back and forth between me and Derek. "What's going on?"

Derek's smile widened as he saw his cousin and moved his way, holding out his hand sideways. "What's up, cuz? I just stopped by to see what you were doing this weekend."

Gabe took the offered palm and they clasped hands, pulling each other into a quick bro hug. I took a few steps back, unsure of what to do or say. I should leave, therefore alleviating any risk that Derek might see something between Gabe and me.

But Derek was having too much fun playing. He jerked his thumb my way and sneered, "Found a Blackburn sullying your block." His gaze moved to me, eyes glittering with malice and lust, a combination that made me furious and sick at the same time. "But she's hot, right cousin? We could probably both take her out for a spin."

I saw the fury and hatred blaze across Gabe's face over Derek's crude suggestion, and I thought to myself... Oh, wow... it's all going to come out now.

Derek turned back toward Gabe, laughing at his suggestion, and I watched as the rage melted right off Gabe's face and to my horror, he started laughing with Derek. "Seriously, dude... even I'm not willing to slum it with a Blackburn, no matter how hot she is."

My heart shriveled up right there. Logically, I knew Gabe didn't mean it and he was merely trying to hide his true feelings for me. But it was a betrayal because this wasn't just about pretending we had nothing—it was his failure to stand up to someone attacking me.

It was immediately unforgivable and no matter how crushed I felt at that moment, it was anger that had me spinning on my heel and walking away from them.

Derek's laugh followed me but I heard nothing from Gabe. I didn't look back and the tears didn't start until I was in my dorm room. I wasn't surprised when no more than ten minutes passed until Gabe was banging on my door.

He barged into my room, scrubbing his hands over his

face as he turned to me. "I'm sorry about Derek. He's an idiot and I had no choice but to play along with him or else I would have outed us."

That hurt far more than it should have. "Derek is a predator and you're a coward." Gabe flinched which meant I'd hit my mark as intended. "You not only stood by while he said vile things about me, you ended up doing the same."

Gabe's voice rose with anger. "You know why I couldn't. If our families found out about us—"

"That's always your excuse," I snapped. "What we are, who we are—it's always hidden and I thought that was the biggest cross I had to bear in this relationship. But it's not. It's the fact that you don't care enough to even defend me."

"Derek was just talking out his ass—"

My voice was eerily quiet, soft with defeat. "Derek was making sexual suggestions, possibly hinting at assault. If you and I were an actual couple, he never would've done that. If that was any other person who didn't know about the rift between our families, you would have kicked their ass for speaking that way about me."

Gabe muttered a curse under his breath because he knew I was right. He was extremely overprotective of me in all ways—except when his family member was the predator.

He reached for my hand, but I pulled it away. "I don't want to be your secret anymore, Gabe."

Expression etched with pain, he said, "Just give it more time, Kat. Please."

I felt the rift growing between us, a chasm widened by

unspoken words, the heavy weight of our secret relationship suddenly unbearable. "I can't do this anymore. It's us, out in the open, or nothing at all. Your choice."

Gabe's jaw locked hard, his hands clenching until his knuckles turned white. "Is this an ultimatum?"

I lifted my chin, unwilling to back down. "It is."

Gabe nodded, his voice raw with restrained emotion. "I guess that's it, then."

The finality of the words hung heavy in the air as the realization that we were over settled in. A strange mix of relief, along with a profound sadness, washed over me.

I reached for the door and opened it. "Goodbye, then."

Gabe didn't reply but walked out. I shut the door behind him, sank to the floor and cried my eyes out.

My cell phone rings and I startle out of the horrible memories I've done my best to not think about. I connect the call, seeing my mom's name on the screen. "Hi, Mom. What's up?"

"Wonderin' how things are gettin' on," she says, her Irish brogue softened with worry.

I glance at the couch and see Sylvie is opening a stack of presents. She's holding up a necklace with a locket charm on it. Gabe helps her with the hinge and when she opens it up, Sylvie gasps. I can't see from here but I assume it's a picture of Alaine when Sylvie throws her arms around Gabe's neck for a long hug.

"It's going great," I tell my mom.

"I'm fair chuffed to hear that," she says upon a contented sigh.

"I'm happy too," I agree softly, so very happy that Sylvie is getting the type of uncle every little girl deserves, some validation that her Mardraggon roots have good in them, and that she has one more person to love her dearly.

CHAPTER 10

Gabe

I'M ADMITTEDLY A workaholic, spending upward of eighty to ninety hours a week devoted to Mardraggon Enterprises. When our family settled in the Kentucky area, a fortuitous marriage with a Scots woman who had a wealth of knowledge about distilling techniques from her homeland forged our family's destiny. Corn was abundant and grapevines were not, so bourbon was where we focused our efforts. Our family was one of the pioneers to use charred oak barrels to age the liquor, which became a defining characteristic of bourbon, and once we refined the process in the nineteenth century—particularly how to bottle it to preserve its quality and authenticity—Mardraggon Spirits Company was formed.

The company grew during the Civil War and we became known for our quality bourbon. We almost went under during Prohibition, the Blackburns doing all they could through political connections to block our ability to obtain medicinal licenses, but we persevered. Our case of Mardraggon Shadow Reserve Barrel was produced in only the second year of Prohibition, another reason it's so valuable.

Post Prohibition, we were among the first distilleries to modernize. We experimented with different aging and production techniques and in 1964 Congress recognized bourbon as a "distinctive product of the United States." That meant it was time for us to go global.

Our family's winery in Saint-Émilion, while lucrative and part of our European legacy, became more of a hobby business, which was the main reason Alaine was allowed free rein with it. By the nineties, Mardraggon Spirits Company had generated billions in revenue and was renamed Mardraggon Enterprises, something my father felt spoke more to our worldwide impact. It was vain, in my opinion.

Regardless, I'm at the helm now and my goal is to make us even bigger and better in the years to come. It's because of our legacy steeped in history that I'm so passionate about my work. I couldn't let Lionel Mardraggon bring it all down and I have zero regrets about ousting him from the board. I've not lost a wink of sleep over cutting him out of my life. What he did to Sylvie was unforgivable and I'll do whatever is necessary to make sure he never has a say in Mardraggon Enterprises ever again.

It's with the knowledge that my work is stressful and

our family is facing some very dark days that the hug Sylvie bestows upon me now fills me in ways I didn't know I needed.

"When can we see each other again?" she asks me.

My eyes lift to Kat standing at the door. She's going to drive Sylvie up to the main house. I offered to do it, but Kat nixed the idea and I'm guessing it's because no one in that family really wants to see me. I've received very little credit for turning my own father in but I'm not surprised. I'm a Mardraggon and should be hated by the Blackburns.

It's that simple.

Kat smiles at Sylvie. "Talk to your dad about the next time you can see your uncle. I'm sure he'll be glad to propose a schedule."

"Did this work for you?" I ask, my eyes locked on Kat. It's been hard to see her here in this apartment, the place we used to meet secretly all those years ago. "Because we can make a standing meeting for us to go over winery plans after I see Sylvie. This time every week is good for me."

Kat's expression is inscrutable. "How about we go through the stuff you brought over tonight so I can get an idea of how much of my involvement will be necessary?"

A not-so-subtle way for her to say she's not sure she wants to spend any length of time around me, either dealing with the winery business or chaperoning my visits with Sylvie. I don't push her on it, though, merely inclining my head.

"Wait here. I'll be back in five minutes. Restroom is through that door…"

Her voice trails off as she realizes she doesn't need to tell me which door leads to the toilet and which one is for her bedroom. I know the exact layout of this little abode, although it looks a lot different than it did eight years ago. Kat has clearly put her touches on it throughout.

Sylvie gives me another hug, thanks me again for the presents, and then they're dashing out the door in their raincoats. When I'm alone, I take my time and walk around the place. Nothing is recognizable from when we snuck in here to be together. I shamelessly open her bedroom door, take in the black wrought iron bed and lacy duvet cover. Strong and feminine, exactly how I'd describe Kat.

I note the hordes of framed pictures—on shelves, tables, walls. All family and friends, Kat always smiling big for the camera. I used to take pictures of her all the time on my phone and they're still there, but in a hidden folder I don't ever look at. I didn't move them there right after we broke up, pulling them up each night and scrolling through them like a lovesick fool. Kat smiling coyly, laughing with gusto, naked on white sheets, slurping spaghetti, lying on a blanket outside, staring up at the trees.

Exiting her room, I head back into the living area. I walk the perimeter, noting the eclectic mix of décor. An art deco floor lamp with a thin, fluted glass shade casting multicolored sparkles, a vibrant Moroccan rug with red and blue geometric patterns, an antique globe with a weathered brass frame and an intricately carved wooden dragon that sits perched on the edge of a bookshelf. All items that have nothing to do with each other and yet seem to all go together somehow. It's a room that would hurt my orderly, conservative brain, yet it's comfortable and warm.

It's a bit torturous looking at something that represents what I couldn't have, knowing that the reason I couldn't have it was because I made the choice to walk away. Kat called me a coward and she might be right, but it doesn't mean I didn't care for her. I wanted us to work and I would have eventually figured out how to make our families okay with it, but she wanted too much, too fast. She never gave me the chance to get it right.

Two weeks after Derek accosted Kat and I'd made the sickening decision to not stick up for her and instead acted cruelly toward her, I was still mired in guilt and the stifling oppression that I'd made a horrible mistake. I hadn't wanted to go but my fraternity brothers pushed me into attending the last home football game of the season. UK is known for its basketball but football was always my sport, so it's not like I wouldn't have fun. I was trying to move on with my life, convinced things would eventually get better.

That I'd stop missing Kat.

It was at the end of the half and my buddies and I were walking back to our seats. We'd tailgated before the game and even though I was only nineteen, I never had a problem purchasing beer or liquor. Partying was the college way of life and I partook.

I wasn't so drunk though that I didn't see Kat standing in line at one of the concession stands. She was beautiful in jeans, furry boots and a white puffy coat with a blue and white UK scarf. Her black hair was loose and her green eyes sparkled with humor as she laughed at... something the guy next to her said.

A man with his arm around her waist. He was tall, athletic and wore glasses that didn't make him look nerdy but somehow like a supermodel, accentuating his good looks. They were a beautiful couple and I was immediately enraged that it took her only two weeks to move on when I'd been wallowing in self-condemnation.

I didn't hesitate. I had enough beer in me to be bold. I told my friends I'd meet them back at the seats and I walked her way.

Her date saw me first and must have understood my intention to talk to her by the expression on my face. He nodded at me and Kat turned, her cheerful smile sliding off when she saw me.

My chest was tight, my pulse hammering as I came to stand beside her in line. "What are you doing here?" I asked.

She looked at me like I was crazy. "Um… watching the football game."

"Can we talk?" I blurted, not daring to look at the man beside her whose arm dropped from her waist.

Kat didn't immediately concede, instead turning to her date. "I'm sorry, Daniel. Do you mind?"

His smile was easy, teeth gleaming and perfectly straight. "Not at all. What do you want?"

"Just a hot dog and a Coke," she replied, going to her tiptoes to place a kiss on his cheek. I couldn't help but think that was to rub it in, but I gritted my teeth and led her away from the line and the crowd to an empty spot on a cinder block wall near some garbage cans.

I turn to face her, ready to fight. "That didn't take you long."

Kat stared at me impassively before glancing over her shoulder. When she brought her attention back to me, it was with sharp eyes and a stubborn set to her chin. "You have no right to even care that I'm seeing someone. You gave up that right when you couldn't be bothered to defend me."

"You didn't give me a chance," I say with frustration. "Just an ultimatum."

"I'd been begging you for months to tell our families. You were never going to do it."

"I would have if—"

"No," she said, shaking her head furiously so that her

black hair tumbled over her shoulders. "Your loyalty is to your family and I can respect that. But there comes a time when you have to stand up for the things you want, and let's be honest, Gabe… you never would've had the spine for it."

She walked away, the noise of the crowd around us fading as I absorbed the gut punch of truth she'd just leveled. I watched her go and a part of me broke as I realized I'd lost something precious, all for the sake of family loyalty.

If only I had the same courage then that I have now. There was never a moment I pondered the choice to turn my father in. Every bit of the loyalty that kept me and Kat apart all those years ago splintered, pulverized, and blew away by my father's actions. He is as good as dead to me and here I am, having more regret than ever over my inaction with Kat.

But that's the past and my future is all kinds of fucked up. Ruminating over what might have been serves no purpose and is nothing but a distraction. I've got to stay focused on Mardraggon Enterprises, especially since I am now in charge of it all.

The door to Kat's apartment opens and she bustles in, shaking off droplets from her hair. She undoes her thin rain jacket and tosses it over a wall hook.

"Are you hungry?" she asks, not in a warm, inviting way but brusquely, to remind me we're still on business time. She moves into the kitchen as I stand from the couch. From the fridge she pulls two bowls and sets them on the small counter that separates the kitchen from the living area.

I lean over as she removes plastic wrap and see chicken salad and fruit. "Looks great."

"Let's talk about the winery and eat at the same time. Sooner we get that done, the sooner you can be on your way."

It rankles me that she can go from being kind enough to offer her apartment for me to meet Sylvie to wanting to kick me out. "We don't have to eat," I say, moving over to my briefcase to grab the documents I brought. "That will save time."

"I went to the trouble to make this, the least you could do is eat," she snaps.

I hold up my hands in surrender, one holding the expansion proposal. "Fine. We'll eat."

"What do you want to drink?" she asks.

"Got any Mardraggon?" I ask, grinning at her slyly.

"Gross. I've got water or Diet Coke."

"Water," I reply, dropping the proposal on the small kitchen table. "Where's the silverware?"

"Drawer to the right of the stove."

We work in silence as we heap chicken salad and fruit onto our plates. At the small table, the proposal is ignored as we eat in silence for a few minutes.

"This is really good," I say in compliment to the chef.

She doesn't reply, merely pulling a strawberry off her fork and into her mouth. That incredibly perfect mouth that I know very well.

I look down at my plate and concentrate on the food.

"The locket you gave Sylvie." I look up to find Kat staring at me intently. "What was on the inside?"

"A picture of her and Alaine taken last year. Alaine was still vibrant and healthy looking. I wanted her to remember her mom in the good days."

It seems a bitter pill to swallow but Kat admits, "That was very thoughtful."

I shrug, stabbing a chunk of chicken. "I love her."

"I know," she replies quietly, then coughs to clear her throat. Her eyes dart down to the proposal. "I assume you're going to summarize that for me."

Nodding, I wipe my mouth with a napkin. Taking the sheaf of documents, I flip it open. "Pages one through five provide an overview of how the winery operates in very simplified form, just to get you up to speed." I turn another page. "On page six, I've got bullet points listing out a variety of things we need to focus on, like some investment opportunities and a new marketing plan, but I want to focus you on page thirteen... expanded distribution."

"Why is that the most important?" Kat asks.

"Because that was what Alaine was working on when she got sick. I want to continue something that was important to her."

Kat stares at me a moment, then nods. "What does expanded distribution mean specifically?"

"Moving deeper into the US market, which we have a small slice of but nothing compared to the European market. We'd have to establish relationships with distributors who specialize in imported wines. There are plenty of small- to medium-sized companies looking for unique offerings to differentiate themselves in a competitive market."

"And how is that done?"

"A seed investment into hiring more staff as well as a specialty company to create targeted marketing campaigns."

Kat has another question, but she seems unsure of how to ask and instead spins her fork in her food. I feel the need to provide her assurances. "You're an expert in the business of horses. I'd have a billion questions if I tried to move into that industry. I expect you're going to have a ton of questions for me so don't hesitate to ask them. If you're to be the go-between for me and Ethan, you need to understand all of this, so ask away."

After taking a sip of water, Kat says, "Okay… fine. What type of money will it take to do this, and what type of money will be generated?"

My smile widens and I point at her, stabbing my finger in the air. "Those are excellent questions. The two most important ones you could ask. I've got it all laid out here on page twenty-seven."

I flip to the appropriate place and scoot my chair around so I can sit closer to her. She pushes her plate back and I put the five-year progression chart before her, showing the initial investment and the expected return over that period.

She studies it thoughtfully before asking, "What other considerations are there? More customers means the need for more wine."

Something inside my chest expands and I easily identify it as pride in Kat. I always knew she was smart as hell, but she's proving that she's the right person for Ethan to have put on this. "Of course, we'll have to increase our production gradually. There's additional acreage we already own with mature vines. It means investing in more barrels, maybe even new technology for the bottling line. We need to ensure that our quality doesn't suffer as we scale up."

For the next two hours, Kat and I discuss the expansion plan and go page by page through the entire proposal. We eat as we talk, and I take a second helping. There's no animosity in the words between us, Kat intently focused on what I'm guessing is now a challenge she wants to conquer.

Standing from the table, Kat stretches with her hands raised far above her head and arches her back. Her T-shirt rides up, exposing barely an inch of skin on her stomach, but the material pulls tight over her breasts. Head tipped back and eyes closed, she can't see me taking visual advantage as my gaze roams over her. She might be an enemy now, but she was absolutely my sexiest mistake.

As her arms drop, I gather up the empty plates that were long ago forgotten after we'd finished eating. I take them to the sink and run water over them, but I don't see a dishwasher, so I just leave them there. Kat follows behind, empty glasses in hand.

"What about the other stuff?" she asks.

"We need to go over it because the new investment opportunities go hand in hand with the expansion plans but it's getting late. I've got an early appointment and you get up earlier than I do."

Kat's eyes flare with surprise.

"What?" I ask with a grin, slightly amused. "I remember you talking about how early your days started when you did training on our summer breaks."

Kat is not amused at the reminder of our time together. Instead, she brushes past me to the door. "Yeah… it's late and we can talk about this stuff some other time."

I follow her, flipping through my calendar on my phone. "How about Thursday at eleven a.m. at my office in Frankfort?"

When Kat opens the door, I see the rain has stopped. She turns to me, hands on her hips. "That won't work for me. You see, I actually work very hard at my job, sunup to sundown."

"As do I," I point out. "I just happen to wear a suit and you wear grubby clothes, but that doesn't make you a harder worker or have less time than me."

She shrugs. "I can meet in the evenings, after eight, since I usually eat dinner with my family."

"Are you being obstinate just to be obstinate?" I ask, genuinely curious, slightly annoyed and again... a little amused.

Kat snorts and I swear I see her lips twitch in what threatens to break into a smile, but she smothers it. "Like I said, any time after eight p.m." She then considers something else. "Except tomorrow. Not free at all."

I nod in understanding. "The Spirits and Saddles Gala?"

It's a charity event where all the bourbon distilleries in the area—and there are a lot—pair up with the horse industry to raise money. It's held at the state fairgrounds in Louisville and there are loads of activities throughout the day but most significantly, bourbon-tasting tents and equine demonstrations inside the indoor arena. Typically, the distilleries each pair up with a farm—usually thoroughbred breeders, but there's a large saddlebred community too—and work together to compete for the most money raised.

She nods. "We're paired up with Bluegrass Barrel Company."

"Hmm," I murmur.

Mardraggon Enterprises is joining with Crescent Meadow, which is the largest horse farm in Kentucky. They breed, train and sell thoroughbreds and have a storied history in the racing community. They've produced numerous successful racehorses that sell for millions of dollars.

Obviously, the best bourbon manufacturer got paired with the best horse farm, but I keep that opinion to myself. I'm not in the mood to have the Hell Kat come out and slice me up with that sharp tongue of hers.

"Let me guess," she drawls, a condescending tone in her voice. "You're paired with Crescent Meadow."

"I'm not sure," I say vaguely, pocketing my phone and pulling out my keys. "Not my bailiwick."

Which is absolutely true. The bailiwick part, although I do know about Crescent Meadows.

My parents typically handled all the social events that Mardraggon Enterprises was involved in. However, times have changed and no one wants to see Lionel Mardraggon at a fundraising function. The board of directors made it clear I need to be in attendance this year.

"Well, figure a time you can meet in the evening again," Kat says as she gestures toward the doorway, a nonverbal cue she really wants me to go.

I step over the threshold and as she starts to shut the door, I put my hand on it to halt her. "Can I see Sylvie when I come back?"

Kat's expression softens slightly. "Yeah… if she's not busy with something else."

"How about day after tomorrow? I'll rearrange my schedule so I can come back, same time."

"Not before eight," she reminds me. "I've still got work to do and I'll be doing lessons or training up until at least six. I cut lessons short today to accommodate you but I can't do that all the time."

"I'll come over to the barn then," I suggest. "Sylvie and I can hang out there under your watchful eye."

"I'll be watching the horses," she replies blandly. "But let me check with Ethan and find out what Sylvie's schedule is day after tomorrow and I'll let you know."

Inclining my head, I hope she hears how grateful I am. No matter what, getting to see Sylvie is paramount. "Thank you. And thanks for dinner too."

"That won't happen again," she asserts with her chin lifted.

Chuckling, I turn away from Kat and trot down the stairs. No, I don't imagine she will invite me to dine with her anytime soon. Despite the moments of levity tonight and our ability to keep things civil as we discussed business, I don't ever forget that she hates my guts and will never forgive me for what I did.

CHAPTER 11

Kat

THE KENTUCKY EXPOSITION Center in Louisville sometimes feels like a home away from home. I've been competing in Freedom Hall at the World Championship Horse Show since I was five. While there aren't green shavings in the arena tonight—a hallmark of the world championships—I still get a thrill standing in this building.

The Spirits and Saddles Gala has been around far longer than I have and usually it's an event my whole family attends. But my parents left for Ireland to visit Mom's family and Wade is at home nursing a spring head cold. Ethan's opting for a quiet night with Marcie and Sylvie and he deserves it. I don't know how the man does it all and I've never been more in awe of my brother than I am now. Just trying to do my regular job of lessons and horse training plus the medical oversight I took off his plate is brutal in terms of time consumption. Add on that I'm now trying to learn about Sylvie's winery and the number of hours I can sleep are dwindling.

But I am getting better at multitasking and managing my day. I've learned how to save my administrative work for evenings at home, rather than trying to cram it into fifteen-minute chunks between lessons. I'm compacting my training sessions to work more efficiently and have even passed some of the lessons on to other instructors. I managed myself so well today, I actually had time to tackle Shadow again and we made three walking laps around the arena with no issues.

It was a job well done and now I'm here to celebrate. Tonight it's just me and Trey, though I haven't seen my brother since we arrived. He's probably off getting busy with Becca Caudill and I'm sure he'll surface at some point.

The gala raises money for local community services across multiple counties, such as volunteer fire departments, libraries and animal shelters. It's held here at the expo center because it's a huge event and there is an obscene amount of money within the bourbon and equine industries. Combined, they account for a $15.5 billion total economic impact with over a billion dollars generated in state and local taxes. To say that this state would flounder without these two powerhouse commercial enterprises is an understatement. The people gathered here tonight to raise money could probably support small, underdeveloped countries on their own.

It's a formal affair and I'm nearly blinded by the glittering jewels dripping off the women. While I'm normally at home in a pair of riding jods and a T-shirt, I do like to dress up on occasion. Tonight I'm wearing a formfitting, full-length gown with a mermaid silhouette. It's adorned with an intricate pattern of leaves in a glossy black finish against a shimmering deep pink background. The bodice is cut asymmetrically with a swath of fabric that drapes over my left shoulder and hangs down my back, which is nearly bare to my tailbone. It's sexy, sophisticated and makes me feel like a different woman, which I don't think is necessarily a bad thing.

I watch the horses being shown in the arena. We have a few of ours on display here, including some yearlings, but the grooms are handling that, leading them around so the folks can appreciate their fancy gaits and elegant necks with heads held high. Part of me is working as I scope out the saddlebreds from other farms coming in. My riders and I will be competing against a number of them over the summer.

After a while, I decide to hit the north wing lobby where the bourbon is displayed. A maze of tasting booths has been set up throughout, some extravagantly decorated to look like old-time speakeasies or elegant bars. The place is packed and I see several people I know in the saddlebred business.

But bourbon and thoroughbreds are king in this state, two enterprises I know very little about. I do, however, like the taste of bourbon so I meander through the booths, deciding to sample from a few smaller distilleries. I have no clue where Mardraggon Enterprises is set up, but I know I'll stay clear of it when I spot it.

For the next half hour, I mingle, taking tiny sips of craft liquor and catching up with old friends. I see Trey and Becca walking around and note she has a piece of hay stuck in her hair, so I'm sure they got down to business in either a horse trailer or stall.

I make my way out of the lobby and down a hallway to a set of bathrooms. I've been diligently drinking water to dilute the alcohol and am not looking forward to wrestling this tight dress up and over my hips.

It is indeed a struggle but I manage to do my business. As I'm washing my hands, I hear the announcer over the speakers calling everyone into Freedom Hall so the final tally of money raised can be reported, followed by boring speeches from some of the richer benefactors. It's their chance to shine and primp under their halo of wealth.

I dry my hands and check my makeup, not in any real hurry. I have no interest in going into the hall to listen to that drivel and will instead take advantage of the distinct lack of lines to try a few more sips of bourbon.

Stepping out of the restroom alcove, I pause a moment to consider where I want to go. The north wing lobby is almost empty, only a few people remaining. I imagine in about half an hour, it will be bustling again and this will turn into a party that won't stop for hours.

"Are you purposely avoiding the Mardraggon booth or avoiding me?" My skin prickles as I recognize Gabe's voice. He's so close, I can feel his breath across my bare shoulder. I turn to see him for the first time tonight and it's unfair how beautiful he is. I'm sure the custom-tailored tuxedo lends a bit of posh to his entire being, but it's his charisma that is enthralling. His honey-colored eyes are without an ounce of shame as he lets his gaze drift down my body and back up again. "And I must say… you clean up well."

I can't tell if that's a compliment or a put-down, but I'm going with the latter since he's a Mardraggon. "Yes, well, not everyone is born with a silver spoon in their mouth."

Gabe tips his head back and laughs. "Oh, come on, Kat. The Blackburns are filthy rich, same as the Mardraggons."

"Except we break our backs for that wealth. We don't sit on gilded thrones and have minions do our work."

"Is that what you think I do?" Gabe asks pensively, tucking his hands into his pockets.

"I really don't care what you do," I say primly. "You

don't interest me at all."

Gabe's eyes flash and darken, and I wonder why that offends him so much. "I imagine being a lowly stable hand makes it nearly impossible for you to comprehend the intricacies of finance and business."

A flush of fury wells within me, because I'm pretty sure he just called me stupid. I have no good comeback to prove my intelligence since I did, in fact, drop out of college and before that, Gabe had to tutor me in math. So I hit him below the belt instead. "Big words coming from someone with a little dick."

The minute the words are out, I'd sell my soul to the devil to pull them back. They're stupid, trite and nowhere near the truth. Gabe Mardraggon is a well-proportioned man in all ways and I just sounded like a toddler hurling nonsensical insults.

I expect him to laugh at me or possibly walk away. I am wholly unprepared for his hands to come to my shoulders before he's pulling me into him and mashing his mouth against mine. I'm so stunned that for a moment, I can't even react and then I'm horrified when my mouth opens and accepts his kiss.

It seems as if flames are licking at my tongue, and oh my God, a tiny moan slips out of my mouth. I feel completely powerless to stop the free fall and that's because this isn't the nineteen-year-old boy who I used to kiss on the down low but rather a powerful man who has learned a thing or two over the years. One hand cups my face, the other grazes down my bare back before latching hard onto my hip to pull me against his tall frame.

His lips leave mine and move to my ear. "Feel that?"

Oh yes... I feel it. As I said, it was an out-and-out lie that he has a small dick. I can't answer him though because his mouth is on my neck and I'm nearly incapacitated by the swiftness of the lust he's induced. An ache between my legs forms and I press against him.

Gabe nibbles his way up to my jaw, feathers his mouth across mine and then lifts his head to peer down at me. "Next time you insult my dick, I'm going to do the same thing to you. So choose your words carefully."

I blink at him stupidly. "What?"

His grin is evil and triumphant. "I didn't realize I could hold such power over you still."

Power over me?

Because...?

It dawns on me what he just said and while the kiss didn't bother me in the slightest, I'm beyond offended that he thinks he can control me. I slap my hands against his chest and shove him hard. While he's got several inches in height and many more pounds of muscle, he's unprepared for my anger or my strength and takes two stumbling steps before he rights himself.

I dramatically wipe my mouth with the back of my hand, snarling, "That was gross."

"You were practically humping my leg," he says dryly. "But if it makes you feel better to say that, you do you."

"Kiss my ass," I snap, again unable to come up with anything to put him in his place. But Gabe isn't a man who's easily knocked down a peg.

I start to turn away, but his hand is on my arm, halting me. It's not tight but gentle. "Kat…"

Glancing back at him, I tug my arm away. "What?"

"I actually have something important to talk about regarding Sylvie."

The kiss is forgotten as is my anger—not just at him, but at myself for responding—because I hear the hesitation in his voice. And as powerful, intelligent and confident as this man is, he sounds near to begging. "What is it?" I ask.

"Sylvie's getting out of school for the summer soon. She told me she doesn't have any major plans, just hanging around the farm, and that your parents might take her to France in August. I was wondering if perhaps I could take her when she gets out of school. I need to check on some things with the winery, and I know she'd like to go back and see her friends—"

"Ethan won't allow it," I say, stopping his speech. It doesn't matter how sweet that offer is, I know my brother.

"I didn't think he'd just let me take her. I was thinking maybe you could come, see the operations, and that will give you the best picture of the winery. You'll understand far more than I could ever teach you."

The idea has merit on so many levels. I'm sure it would help me and ultimately Ethan when making decisions if I knew what we were actually working so hard for but more than anything, Sylvie has been missing her homeland so much and she's been so brave with all the horrible things that have happened to her.

"I'm so busy, Gabe. I don't know that I can take the time—"

"Will you just think about it and talk to Ethan? I don't know what it would take to turn your duties over to someone else, but if you could manage that, we could do a five-day trip. We'll take one of the Mardraggon jets—"

"We have our own jet," I feel the need to say, which is something he already knows.

"Not as fast as ours though," he replies with a smirk.

I have to force myself not to respond. It's that boyish smile that made me realize back in college that he wasn't the horrible monster we thought all Mardraggons were bred to be.

"I'll talk to Ethan. It might be that someone else has to go other than me." Although I'm not sure who that would be. Trey and Wade are as busy as I am.

"Okay… thank you for considering it." His eyes

move over me one more long, luxurious time and he nods. "Enjoy the rest of your evening."

Gabe steps out from the alcove and disappears around the corner, presumably heading to Freedom Hall.

I lean back against the wall, touching my fingertips to my lips that still tingle from his kiss.

CHAPTER 12

Gabe

I CUT AWAY from Freedom Hall, having no desire to be around people or listen to boring speeches. I'm feeling edgy, out of control, and nothing settles those feelings like alcohol. It's a good thing I know just where to get such a commodity.

The Mardraggon booth is a large U-shaped bar made of hand-carved cherrywood with attached swivel stools along the three sides. There's a top overhang with pendant lighting at the back of the bar, in front of which stands a bartender in an elegant tuxedo. Upon a single shelf sits a bottle of every brand of bourbon we currently produce, each one with its own light shining from underneath to accentuate the bourbon's rich amber hues, making the liquid within the bottles shimmer enticingly.

I believe I saw a report come across my email about the cost of constructing this temporary bar for the Spirits and Saddles Gala, and it was close to fifty thousand dollars. It's going to be disassembled after this event and put into storage, probably never to be used again. Next year, for the same charity event, Mardraggon Enterprises will do something different but no less costly. It's a fine example of just how much money we have and how much is acceptable to spend to market our product.

Technically, the event is just for people to sample the variety of Kentucky bourbons available, but you can also get a full drink—one or two fingers, whichever you prefer.

The bartender sees me, knows exactly who I am, and moves my way as soon as I take a stool at the middle of the bar. There's no one else here and very few people linger in the lobby, since everyone made their way into Freedom Hall for the speeches.

I expect that's where Kat has gone and then hate myself for even spending a moment of thought on her. She's the current reason I'm here and saying to the bartender, "Give me the Copper Still Reserve, neat."

He nods and bows slightly, as if I'm royalty. "Right away, Mr. Mardraggon."

I drum my fingers on the polished wood surface and when the crystal glass slides into my line of sight, I mutter my thanks.

I don't have to pay for this, but I pull a twenty out of my wallet and hand it to him for a tip. I ignore his effusive gratitude, pick up the glass and pull a long sip into my mouth. The warm rush over my palate and into my stomach provides a quelling effect and I sigh with satisfaction.

Someone approaches and takes the stool two down from me, but I don't look that way. I have no desire to engage in niceties or meaningless conversation. It would most likely be someone fawning over the privilege of having the chairman of the board of Mardraggon Enterprises to talk to or someone who wants to talk about my father.

"I'll take the Mardraggon 1921 Shadow Reserve."

The hair rises on the back of my neck as I recognize the voice but it's the request for the rare bourbon that has me turning on my stool.

"I'm sorry, sir," the bartender says solicitously, "but we only have our Copper Still Reserve, Golden Rye Legacy and Rebel's Toast for tasting tonight."

It's the blond thug, Kravitz, who came to my house yesterday but I don't see his cohort around. Frankly, I'd put them out of my mind, thinking the request brazen but lacking validity. I have more important things to worry about but the fact the big man is sitting two stools down at an invitation-only gala has me reconsidering. This is no coincidence. He's clearly got connections.

Turning to face me, Kravitz bestows a smile before twisting back to the bartender. "I'll try the Rebel's Toast."

I'm silent as a small tasting cup is prepared, my eyes

never leaving the guy. He watches the bourbon being poured and when it's offered to him, he holds up the clear plastic cup that holds less than half an ounce. He sniffs it almost delicately, then tilts it back. It's a bourbon drinker I'm watching as he holds the liquid in his mouth to savor, eyes closing slightly before swallowing.

The man hums in approval, looks to me and says, "That's very good. Kudos." He then slides his gaze to the bartender. "I'll take a double."

"No, he won't." The steely edge to my voice has the bartender's head whipping my way before he steps backward as a silent indication he's not going to serve this man per my command.

Kravitz inclines his head as I rise from my stool, looking neither flustered nor affronted. I leave the rest of my drink untouched and walk away from the Mardraggon booth, knowing damn well the man will follow me. He's not here for the 1921 Shadow Reserve, the Rebel's Toast or anything other than a second attempt to try to intimidate me.

I move through the nearly empty exhibit hall, keeping my eyes averted from the handful of people taking advantage of the lack of lines at the open bourbon booths. I walk right out the door, hang a left and move into the shadows because no one needs to witness this conversation.

The evening is cool but I feel flushed, and not in a good way.

Not in the way I felt ten minutes ago kissing Kat.

I hear the scrape of shoes and when I turn to face Kravitz, he's lighting a cigarette. Blowing out a plume of smoke my way, his eyes pin on me. Luckily, the wind catches the foul odor and it drifts away before I have to smell it.

"What are you doing here?" I ask.

The man tucks one hand in his pocket and shrugs. "Enjoying the festivities. Interesting charity gala."

Not a direct answer to my question and I learned long ago not to waste my time on silly, petty games. I start to move past the man to head back into the building. "I've got more important things—"

"I'm here to provide incentive for you to get that case of bourbon for us."

I halt, turn to face the man. He's not in a rush and takes another drag off his cigarette, smoke pouring out of his mouth as he says, "I paid a visit to your father today."

My body tenses but past that tiny bit of wariness, I can't figure out how that makes me feel. There's an implied threat but I'm not sure I really care. Every day that passes, it's not antipathy I feel for my father but raw anger brewing hotter because of the things he's done. As a result, I can't say that I have a single concern for his safety, health or welfare. "And?" I drawl flatly.

The blond man stares at me a long moment before saying, "It was impressed upon him the need to turn over that case of bourbon."

Nothing on my face gives away alarm because it's not alarm I'm feeling. More curiosity. "And exactly how did you do that?"

He chuckles. "Oh, I'm sure you can figure it out. Your dad wasn't moved by our request though."

"That's because he doesn't have the authority."

Kravitz nods, taking another drag from his cigarette. "Yes, Mr. Rafferty said as much, but we had to be sure. He knows you're the one who turned your dad into the police as well as orchestrated his removal as chairman of the board. It's also clear you don't care if we hurt him."

My smile is mirthless. "I'm glad you understand. I don't give a shit what you do to my father."

"What about your mother, though?" The man's lips peel back in a vicious smile.

A pit forms in my stomach because while I don't care what happens to my dad, I obviously don't want my mother hurt.

I can't let them know that though. They can never know she would potentially be a weakness. "My mother has chosen to side with my father. I have broken all ties with both of them, so if you're trying to get to me through them, it's a waste of your time."

He takes another drag, tossing the butt onto the

concrete and crushing it with the toe of his shoe. He blows out smoke and then pins me with a cold look. "I guess that makes you our primary target then. Pity… so much easier to send a message when we know you have someone to care about. I guess we'll be seeing *you* next Tuesday."

For a moment, I have no clue what he means about next Tuesday, but then I remember they said they would come back in one week. I had so thoroughly dismissed their demand as ludicrous, I never thought they would follow up. "Don't bother. I won't have that case."

"We'll still come by and have a talk. I'm sure we'll be able to come to an understanding."

The man starts to walk away but I stop him with my next question. "I don't understand why your boss doesn't get the equivalent of money from Lionel. He's good for it."

Kravitz turns back to me. "Yes, we know your father has plenty of money. Mr. Rafferty has plenty of that too. He has more than he knows what to do with. But he loves to collect things and that case of Shadow Reserve Barrel is what he wants. It's what he was promised."

I'm getting frustrated with how dim this guy is. "Again, my dad bet something he doesn't own. It wasn't his to wager."

"Ownership doesn't matter. Especially when you have the ability to produce it."

Un-fucking-believable. "You better come at me with something more than threats."

The man bobs his head. "Challenge accepted. See you Tuesday."

I don't say anything else and there's no need for me to argue with him further. I watch as he melts into the darkness, briefly considering whether I should call the police. But I'm not even sure what I would say. Nothing criminal has been done at this point.

With a frustrated sigh, I pull out my phone and dial my mother. When she answers, I can tell she's distressed. "Gabe, I'm so glad you called. A man just came to see your father. They went into his office to talk and when he left, I found Lionel bleeding. The man punched him several times."

"Did they threaten you?" I ask.

"No, why would they? What's going on? Your father won't tell me anything."

Typical. But I'm grateful he never shared with her his plan to murder Sylvie. At this point, given her utter devotion to the man, I'm not so sure she wouldn't have gone along with it.

I decide to fill her in on the truth. "Your husband has apparently bet the 1921 Shadow Reserve case of bourbon in a game of high-stakes poker. He lost and now they want payment."

My mother scoffs in that imperious tone that only

she can seem to carry. "That's ridiculous. Your father doesn't play poker. It's such a crass game."

"No offense, Mother, but I'm realizing these days that you don't really know the man at all. I'm sure you thought he would never try to kill Sylvie either."

My mother gasps, outrage in her tone. "He did not do that and it's a horrible accusation you've made."

There's no sense trying to talk sense into her. "Mother… I'm telling you that you have attached yourself to somebody who does not deserve your loyalty. If I were you, I would hire some protection. That man might come back and he might bring others with him."

I don't wait for her response but hang up, knowing I've done the only duty I'm required to do for her.

I step through the glass doors back into the exhibit hall lobby. The crowd is now pouring back in from Freedom Hall and the liquor booths are filling up. This gala will go on for several more hours, people getting drunk as only Kentuckians can do when free bourbon is being offered.

I scan the crowd for Kat, looking for that formfitting and sexy-as-hell dress she's wearing. The kiss we shared was scorching and while I don't like the fact that she had a physical effect on me, I'm absolutely triumphant that she felt the same. I saw it in her eyes. That woman was wound tight when my mouth lifted from hers and I wonder if I could get her into bed. Maybe nothing more than a hookup, but it would definitely take the edge off.

I don't see her, but there are a ton of gorgeous women around. Some I know, some I don't, any one of them I could have in my bed tonight.

Sadly… horrifically… I realize it's only Kat I want. She's not only the sexiest woman I have ever been with, we're cemented by the connection we once shared. For that glorious year, she was mine, and I have to admit it was the happiest time of my life. Losing her was the lowest.

But I've moved on and a hookup with the Hell Kat is a terrible idea. Besides, she's just as likely to cut off my balls as she is to stroke them. I need to leave the idea of Kat Blackburn far behind.

I do the next best thing and head back to the Mardraggon booth to finish my drink, knowing I'm going to order another.

CHAPTER 13

Kat

I

T'S NOT QUITE dusk as I pull up to Gabe's sprawling new mansion, but every single interior light is turned on, as is the outdoor landscape lighting, making the house glow warmer than the sinking sun. The classic terra-cotta brick with stark white accents provide a sharp contrast to the early-evening hues of blue and pink. The front is framed by fluted columns rising from stone bases to support a gabled portico large enough to hold three cars side by side. I park on a herringbone pattern of brick paving as Sylvie leans forward in the passenger seat and practically shrieks. "Oh, wow… look at that house."

Indeed.

I gave Gabe a lot of shit about buying something so grandiose, but one cannot deny its beauty. I can't help but smile at Sylvie's enthusiasm, as she's been practically bouncing in the seat with excitement to see her uncle. The entire drive here, it's been a running litany of chatter filling the car. If I had to name an emotion I'm feeling right now, regrettably, I'm looking forward to seeing Gabe and I have no clue why. I'm still angry that he kissed me three nights ago at the gala.

I have to remind myself that I am here to discuss business. There are only two things relevant to this visit—for Sylvie to see her uncle, who is so important to her, and for Gabe to go over an offer by an investor to fund the expansion. Other than that, there should be nothing even remotely interesting to me and if anything, I should hate being around him.

My Jeep is barely in park before Sylvie's tossing the door open and scrambling out. "Come on, Aunt Kat."

I grin as I follow, thoroughly warmed by the way she calls me *aunt*. I've only held this title a few months now, but it's opened inside me a love I never knew I could have for a child. I've never thought I'd make a particularly good mother, but Sylvie makes me rethink that. Granted, I work with kids on a daily basis, but teaching them how to ride horses doesn't necessarily translate into maternal instincts.

Sylvie, however, makes me think otherwise because she's so damn easy to love.

The door swings open before we make it onto the portico and there stands Gabe dressed casually in a pair of cargo shorts and a navy T-shirt. I haven't seen him dress like this since our college days and he sure as hell looks boyish enough right now with a whip of his blond hair hanging over his forehead. His molten expression is guarded as his eyes come to me first and then warm with welcome when they land on Sylvie. She throws herself into his arms and he hugs her tightly.

"Your house is amazing," Sylvie gushes, having seen nothing but the exterior at this point.

Chuckling, Gabe puts his arm around her shoulders and guides her inside without casting a backward glance at me. I know I'm invited to follow along because technically, I'm still a chaperone. Ethan's not prepared to let Sylvie have alone time with her uncle quite yet.

I enter behind them, closing the door. Gabe leads his niece through the foyer into the formal living area. "I'll give you the grand tour."

Sylvie's head swivels as she looks around the opulent room. She moves to the grand piano that sits atop the circular dais and touches a few of the keys. "If you want to continue lessons," Gabe says to his niece, "I'll be glad to set them up."

I'm stunned by this revelation. "You play piano?"

Sylvie nods with a toothy grin. "Started when I was four."

How did we not know that?

As Sylvie walks around the living area, I take a moment to really soak in the décor. It's sophisticated yet looks homey at the same time, and *homey* is the last word I'd use to describe Gabe. In fact, it's completely impossible for me to envision Gabe in such an environment but what do I know. This is his home now. Maybe he's changed.

Sylvie is as shocked as I am by how beautiful the house is. Such a stark contrast to the cold contemporary feel of Lionel and Rosemund's house, and yet also completely different from the Blackburns' historical home.

Gabe takes Sylvie through each room, culminating on the top floor where the bedrooms are located. I'm shocked when he takes us into the master bedroom as I didn't think he would share that personal side of himself with me in tow.

My mouth is totally agape when we walk in and I know I'll never see as beautiful a bedroom as this one. Three exterior walls are nothing but massive bay windows with white shutters and I can only imagine how bright this room is at midday. What's most shocking is that the room is filled with plants of all types, from small trailing vines to young trees in large pots. They're all healthy and some are budding with flowers and I refuse for a second to believe that Gabe takes care of them himself. I'm not ready to admit he might have normal talents.

"Isn't this room amazing?" Sylvie asks me as she gazes out one of the windows.

I glance at Gabe who leans against the doorjamb

watching. "It's definitely… tranquil," I admit.

We move down a long hall to look at some of the guest rooms. Gabe opens a door to a room, motioning me and Sylvie in. "I thought that maybe one day, if you're allowed to come stay here with me for a visit, this could be your room."

Sylvie gasps as she enters and I see why. It's a little girl's dream.

It's not overtly feminine but it fits Sylvie. The room is anchored by a wrought iron bed, dressed in layers of puffy white bedding that looks as soft as a cloud. A luxurious chandelier with crystal droplets casts a soft glow, enhancing the room's warm taupe walls. Flanking the bed are nightstands, topped with crystal lamps and a circular, off-white lounge chair nestles in the corner. Along another wall is a desk that sits atop a zebra-print rug, which is exactly the dash of whimsy that Sylvie would want if she were to ask.

"I bought this place fully furnished and I'm guessing they had daughters."

Sylvie's smile wanes a bit. "I don't think my dad will let me stay anytime soon."

"That's understandable," Gabe says, and I do a double take his way. The fact he'd validate Ethan's feelings is astounding and well… appreciated. His eyes flick to me briefly before he says, "Well, maybe your aunt Kat can stay overnight with you?"

My stomach flutters because while I'm sure he's talking about only in my capacity as a chaperone, for a fleeting moment, I wonder what it would be like if circumstances were different. What would it be like to lie in that big bed of his? Have his skills as a lover grown over time? Although I admit, he was damn good when he was younger.

Sylvie rounds on me. "Would you stay over here, Aunt Kat?"

"I don't know," I say hesitantly and her smile falters, so I hastily amend, "I'm sure we can work out something."

"Can Renault stay?" Sylvie asks as she glances back to her uncle. Renault is her dog that she had in France and Gabe worked to bring here to the States for her.

"Always," Gabe says easily.

The house is so enormous it takes almost half an hour to see everything and then we're walking out onto the back patio along a garden path to an enormous building of iron and glass.

"What is that?" Sylvie asks.

"The pool house," Gabe says. "You did bring your bathing suit, didn't you?"

She did indeed because I told her to pack it. Sylvie, however, presumed Gabe had a run-of-the-mill, in-ground pool, not a gorgeous Olympic-size indoor pool.

"Wow," Sylvie exclaims as she rushes inside, leaving

Gabe and me to follow.

"Aren't you even the slightest bit embarrassed how ostentatious all of this is?" I ask as we stand shoulder to shoulder, watching Sylvie traverse the custom tilework that surrounds the pool. I know I asked him something like that once before, completely nasty and condescending.

God help me… now I seem to be teasing.

"Not at all," he says with a grin.

Gabe shows us an upstairs living area above the pool, the pungent smell of chemicals not as strong up there. It has a balcony that looks over rolling hills all bordered by white fencing and in the distance atop a ridge sits a beautiful barn that I'd estimate could hold eight horses. "Maybe you can have a horse here one day if you decide you want to ride," Gabe says.

"How about I take a lesson if you take a lesson?" Sylvie asks him, her eyes twinkling mischievously.

I'm completely caught off guard by her offer to Gabe as Sylvie has been adamantly opposed to riding. It's been a sore spot with Ethan—he believes every Blackburn has equine DNA in their blood. She's admittedly been afraid and hesitant but she's spent a lot of time in the barn lately, so maybe she's getting used to the idea.

Gabe's eyes slide to me. "Is your aunt Kat willing to teach us both how to ride?"

I smile at him tartly. "For Sylvie, absolutely. For you,

158

it will cost."

Gabe chuckles. "Fair enough."

We head back to the house and Gabe says, "I was just going to order some Chinese food for us. Sound good?"

"Can I swim first?" Sylvie asks.

Gabe looks to me and I shrug. "Sure. Gabe and I can go over winery stuff while you swim, then we'll eat."

Sylvie scrambles for the bag she brought in. "I'm going to get dressed in my room."

I start to correct her but then stop myself. This is exciting to her and I can never forget that Gabe is the closest thing Sylvie has to her mother. And if I were to guess, there will come a day when Sylvie will have full access to her uncle. It's just not for me to say when.

When Sylvie disappears up the staircase, I turn to Gabe. "I have some good news for you."

One eyebrow arches high. "Since when does a Blackburn give a Mardraggon good news?"

My lips twitch, but I press on. "Ethan is going to let Sylvie go to France with you as soon as school is out. Our parents will still take her in August, but she's really homesick and so he thinks this will be great for her."

"Really?" Gabe exclaims. "I didn't think he'd ever go for it."

Neither did I, to be honest. It was a hard sell and tempers rose around the dinner table last night. I waited

159

until after we'd all eaten and Sylvie had gone upstairs to shower and lay out her clothes for the school day. That gave me about half an hour of privacy to get the group's collective opinion, because I knew Ethan wouldn't make a decision without running it by everyone.

"Gabe has requested that he be allowed to take Sylvie back to Saint-Émilion when she gets out of school." Mouths opened and glares formed, but I hastily added, "Obviously, I would go along as a chaperone and it would give me a better idea of how the winery operates."

Ethan was silent, but that is his way. If he wasn't in flat-out, one-word denial, he was thinking. Marcie reached over and put her hand on his, showing that she would support his decision regardless. My mom was bothered that she wouldn't have the first opportunity to take Sylvie to France and immediately started talking to my dad about canceling their other trip they had already planned and paid for which conflicts with their ability to take her now instead of in August. Trey and Wade were the ones who blew up, immediately fueling the flames and, in a way, attacking me.

"There's no way that asshole is allowed to take Sylvie out of the country," Wade snapped. "Are you crazy? He's Mardraggon."

"He can't be trusted," Trey added. "None of them can be. How could you even bring something like this to the table for consideration?"

They raged and cursed, but a sharp look from our mom ended their protests. Still, it didn't stop them from calling me ten kinds of stupid for even thinking it. Throughout it all I didn't say a word, just waited for them to run out of steam and when they finished, I reiterated my reasoning. "Gabe has shown his loyalty is to Sylvie, not the Mardraggon family. Sylvie loves him deeply and needs this relationship because he's the last tie to her mom. She's homesick and she's going to be perfectly safe with me along."

Ethan sat back and pondered it all.

When my bonehead brothers finally shut up, I realized it wasn't just me I was defending in my reasoning for letting her go but also Gabe. Something in me had softened toward him—not as a man who I had a prior relationship with but a human being who was desperately trying to hold on to a bond with his niece because he cares so much for her.

I continued laying it all out there, mostly for Trey and Wade's benefit, so I looked directly at them. "I don't feel like I should have to remind you, but apparently I do because you two are too dense. Gabe turned his father in to the police and is the one person who guaranteed Sylvie's safety. On top of that, he removed the death clause from the trust agreement, which not only further guarantees her safety, but in case you didn't figure it out, it removed the winery from the Mardraggon legacy. That business has been in their family for over a hundred years and he basically gave it to the Blackburns. He's busting his ass to make it better for Sylvie and he gets nothing from that. So quit trying to paint him as a villain when in this instance, he's not."

Trey and Wade kept their mouths shut but I could tell they didn't like those reminders. My parents looked stunned and then pensive.

But they didn't matter. I turned to Ethan. "What do you think?"

He didn't answer and I had to suppress a grin when he turned to Marcie. "What do you think?"

She immediately shook her head and held out her palms. "Oh, no you don't. That's not my decision."

"Your opinion matters to me," he said, taking one of her hands in his. "Give it to me straight."

Marcie's eyes softened and she smiled at Ethan. She then glanced around the table at everyone, her gaze holding the longest on my brothers before she said, "I think it's important to let Sylvie have a relationship with Gabe and not just a surface relationship. I think it needs to be fostered... deepened, even. Everything that Kat said is true and he deserves our trust, I think. But more importantly, Gabe is the last representation that Sylvie has of her mother. You can't take that from her."

Ethan nodded and I could tell by the expression on his face that was exactly what he was thinking. "She's really homesick for France and she deserves some fun and goodness right now." He glanced over to my parents. "I'm sorry. I know you want to take her and you still should at the end of the summer, but I think it would be great if she went now." Ethan then brought his attention to me. "But you'd have to go, Kat. You made a compelling argument that Gabe has earned some trust, but he doesn't have my full level and I'm not sure he ever will."

I was happy that Ethan decided to let Sylvie go and there was one thing he and I were absolutely aligned on. I wasn't sure Gabe would ever have my full trust either, and that's not just because of his last name.

"And you'll be coming with Sylvie and me?" Gabe asks.

And… is his voice huskier than normal? I shake off that notion. "Yeah, you still need a chaperone."

Gabe snorts in amusement, shaking his head but then when his eyes land on me, they're warm and filled with gratitude. "Kat, this—thank you. It means a lot that you managed this."

I cross my arms, leaning against the wall. "Sylvie deserves this and it's important to her. We're all working in her best interests."

Gabe steps closer, his presence overwhelming. "And what about you? Going to France with me—this isn't a simple decision."

I avoid his gaze, focusing instead on the patterns in

the wood grain of the parquet flooring. "I've arranged for my brothers to cover for me at the farm. It's handled."

"That's not what I asked." Curiosity lifts my head to meet his eyes. "Are you okay with this? With us being there together?"

I don't like the softness in his voice or the promise in those words. Or maybe I don't like imagining such things. "There is no us," I say flatly.

The corner of his mouth curves upward and he actually taunts me. "Didn't seem that way the other night."

A sound rattles in my throat, dismissively haughty. "It was just a kiss, not that good and already forgotten."

Stroking a thumb along his chin, he murmurs, "Not the way I remember it. Maybe you need a reminder."

"Maybe you need a swift kick to the balls if you try it," I reply sweetly, even fluttering my eyelashes. My words have bite and determination, but I can tell by the way he's looking at me that he knows as well as I do that if he kissed me, I'd go all in.

Luckily, Sylvie's footsteps pound down the stairs. We both turn to see her coming at breakneck speed with a towel slung over her shoulder. She's sporting a cute yellow bathing suit with white polka dots and ruffles along the shoulders and hips. "Let's go swimming."

"Let's do it," Gabe says, slinging his arm over her shoulders. He walks her toward the back patio door that will lead to the pool path and I follow along. I watch as they chat easily, Sylvie's smile as bright as her swimsuit and that makes having to deal with Gabe Mardraggon very easy.

CHAPTER 14

Gabe

WALKING THROUGH THE main floor of my home, I switch lights off as I prepare to go up to my bedroom. It's nowhere near bedtime and I still have a lot of work to do, but I have found the master suite to be extremely comfortable. I've taken to doing evening work sitting atop the big four-poster bed with my laptop propped before me. In the kitchen, I grab a bottle of water and in the pantry a bag of peanuts to snack on. My phone chimes in my pocket and I pull it out to see that Kat has texted again.

I ignore the beating of my pulse that happens every time I get a text, call or email from the woman. Over the past handful of days, we've settled into a routine that includes daily contact. If she's not asking questions about something she's read in the mountain of paperwork I've given her about the winery, she's reporting on Sylvie. This is extra special as she's doing so of her own accord, and it speaks to Kat's kind heart, despite years of hard feelings between us.

Today I've had a barrage of questions about what to pack for our trip, which occurs in four days. Sylvie gets out of school on Friday, and we're scheduled to load up on the Mardraggon jet Saturday morning.

I flip to the text thread and smile at Kat's question. *Even though we're taking a private jet, I still need to bring my passport, correct?*

Chuckling, I can't help but think it's utterly adorable that Kat knows nothing about international travel. It's not that I think she's unsophisticated in those ways because she comes from a very sophisticated family. It's just that those things have never been important to her before so she doesn't know about them. I grew up jetting all over the world and although Kat's family had the means to do that, all the Blackburn kids were working the farm probably from the time they could walk.

I set the water and peanuts down on the counter to free my hands for a reply. *Yes. You need your passport. Still have to go through customs.*

The three round dots indicate she's responding and I wait patiently.

Or rather impatiently.

You never know what you're going to get with our exchanges. Sometimes our texts can devolve quickly into an argument or we'll end up teasing each other like the days of old. It lends a thrill to our communications because together we are unpredictable as hell.

Her response is neither though: *Thx.*

Shrugging, I pocket my phone and reach for my snacks when the doorbell rings.

My eyes drift over to the digital clock on the built-in double oven and I see it's just after nine p.m. I've been expecting that doorbell to ring from the moment I arrived home a few hours ago and I even debated whether I would answer or ignore it when it finally happened.

But I'm not one to push my problems aside, so I've already planned out in my mind how this will go down.

Leaving the snack behind, I move through the kitchen that opens into the formal living area, which in turn leads into the foyer. I reach the double front doors and take a breath before grabbing the knob on the left and opening it, knowing damn well who's on the other side.

It's Tuesday night and as promised, Clinton Rafferty's goons are standing on the bottom step under the portico. They didn't pull their SUV underneath but rather left it sitting back farther in the driveway facing us, the headlights on and the engine running. It's the same two men who originally visited me a week ago—Kravitz and Bellamy—although I doubt those are their real names. The blond, Kravitz, was at the Spirits and Saddles Gala last week and he nods to me like we're old friends.

I don't open the door all the way but just enough

that only half my body is visible to them with barely my head and chest sticking out. I hope my message is clear— I don't have any intention of engaging in a lengthy conversation and they're not coming inside my home. "I told you not to bother coming here, that it would be a waste of your time."

Kravitz flashes me a genial smile. "Yes, you did say that, just as I told you I was still coming. I feel I must again impress upon you the urgency by which you should turn over Mr. Rafferty's winnings. He's not known for his patience."

I'd looked up Clinton Rafferty and as expected, I learned that he's a well-respected businessman. Not a surprise—his standing in the business community makes it very easy to deny accusations he's sending thugs out to collect illegal poker winnings. The man was born and raised in Louisville, attended the University of Louisville where he earned a degree in business administration, which laid the groundwork for his future endeavors in the corporate world. I easily found online that he's the founder and CEO of Rafferty Holdings, a conglomerate with interests in a variety of sectors including real estate, hospitality and entertainment. Most of his money is in developing high-profile commercial properties and luxury residential units that have significantly contribut-ed to urban revitalization projects across Louisville, making him a community hero of sorts. No one would ever dare think him capable of extortion and I'm sure he's confident enough that no one will ever buck under the threat of harm.

His high standing in the community also means he's got cops in his back pocket, which I'm confident is how he knew I was the one who turned in my father. That has not been made public yet although select friends and extended family know what I did.

I'm not his typical victim, though. "You can tell Mr. Rafferty to go fuck himself."

That does nothing to rattle either of the men and they both maintain bland smiles. "How about we come inside and discuss this matter?" Bellamy suggests.

I reach over to the baseball bat I had leaned against the wall on the right side of the door and hold it so it's visible. "I think we'll stay right where we are."

Kravitz chuckles as he eyeballs my weapon. "A baseball bat? Is that supposed to scare us?" He pulls aside his suit jacket, revealing a gun tucked in a chest holster. He doesn't need to say anything because his message is that the gun trumps the bat every time.

He's not wrong and I don't bother showing him the pistol I have tucked into the back waistband of my jeans. Instead, I give him a lackadaisical smile and toss the bat onto the ground at his feet. I reach behind the door one more time and grab the shotgun I'd leaned there previously. I open the left door completely and hold the gun across my body. "I've got more than a baseball bat. Take one step closer and you're going to see just how good of a shot I am."

Kravitz holds out his arms in the universal sign that he means no harm, which is a fucking lie. He laughs—an easy-going sound completely at odds with the seriousness of this meeting. "We're just here for what's ours because it's time to pay up. We'd like that to happen without things getting messy."

"I'm getting blue in the face repeating this but I'll say it again… the bourbon is not mine to give. It belongs to Mardraggon Enterprises. Even if it were mine to give, I'm not covering my father's debt. He's on his own." My voice is cold, steady, and there should be no doubt in their minds they're getting nowhere with me.

Bellamy steps forward, his face a hard mask of anger. "Mr. Rafferty won't be happy about this. He expects his winnings."

"And he can take that up with the entire board of directors if he wants. I'll even facilitate a meeting. He's not getting anything from me though."

Kravitz remains silent, a smirk on his face, but Bellamy is incensed I'm not quavering in fear. "You're making a big mistake. Mr. Rafferty isn't someone you want as an enemy."

"Neither am I," I retort, my voice firm as I shift the shotgun in my grip, emphasizing the urgency of my command. "Now, I am telling you to get off my property. I'm not sure if either of you have ever heard of the Castle Doctrine, but it gives me the right to defend my property with deadly force if necessary. However, rather than just shoot the two of you, I invited someone else over to make sure the message is clear you're not welcome here anymore."

Bellamy frowns and Kravitz tenses as someone melts out of the shadows from his right.

A Shelby County deputy sheriff. "Gentlemen, I'm Deputy Chris Parton. Mr. Mardraggon asked me to stop by as he anticipated you might come onto his property without permission. While he's well within his right to defend his ground, I'm hoping I can convince you gentlemen to leave peaceably."

I keep my expression passive but it's hard not to laugh at the disgruntled looks on both of the thugs' faces. I can see they're stunned that I'd actually call the police on them and I'm guessing Rafferty chooses his victims wisely. In other words, those who aren't going to fight against his collection efforts.

I'm not normally one who would run to the police for help with private matters, but Chris is my cousin on my mother's side. He happens to be off duty tonight but when I explained to him what was happening, he had no problem in slipping on his uniform to come over to lend an air of credibility that I'm not kidding when I say I won't be engaging with these people anymore.

It's my hope that Chris's authority will get the message back to Clinton Rafferty that I am not his way in to that debt my father owes.

For a moment, it looks like Bellamy might want to argue but Kravitz merely nods and takes a few steps back.

He looks to Chris and then to me. While his tone is polite, his eyes promise me that this is far from over. "Have a good evening, Mr. Mardraggon. I'm sure we'll run into each other again."

"I hope that's not a threat," Chris says.

Kravitz is cool as a cucumber, making him the more dangerous of the two men. He gives a slight bow toward my cousin. "Not at all, Deputy. Just being polite."

The men walk to the SUV and we watch as they back down the driveway, rather than pulling through the circular drive under the portico. It's well calculated so that we can't see their license plate.

Chris turns to me and we shake hands. "You all right?"

"Yeah, man. Thank you for coming. Hopefully that will be enough to keep them away."

Chris nods. "Hey listen… I'm really sorry about this mess with Lionel. Is Aunt Rosemund doing okay?"

"She's refusing to take any of this seriously. Has her head stuck in the sand. She doesn't believe the charges against him."

"You want me to give her a call?"

It's a nice offer. "That would be great. I've tried to warn her about these guys, but she doesn't believe they'll do anything. She doesn't understand the threat. She thinks they've moved on to me and she's probably right, but you never know."

Chris jerks his head down the driveway. "They pulled in straight and backed out so I couldn't see the license plate."

"Yeah, I thought about that. If they come back, I'll walk out there and look at it myself."

Chris frowns at me with worry. "Not a good idea. If they come back, don't answer the door. Just call us. Those guys had guns and I don't think they're afraid to use them."

"Not afraid to use mine either," I counter. "But I understand what you're saying."

Chris offers his hand and rather than shake it, we clasp briefly before pulling each other into a half hug. "I'm proud of you for turning Lionel in," he says. "That took guts. I know the Mardraggon side of your family likes to stick together."

Being from my mother's side, Chris has never been embroiled in the nasty underbelly of what it means to be a Mardraggon, but he's a local and knows what everyone else knows. Our loyalties run deep.

Except when my niece is threatened. "It was easy.

174

There was really no choice in turning him in."

"I hear you. Just be careful with these goons." He throws his thumb over his shoulder. "I'll get going. Want to shoot clays sometime?"

"Absolutely. I'll text you and we'll set a date. I'm leaving for France for a business trip on Saturday but maybe the week after?"

"Let's do it."

Chris disappears around the corner of the house where a four-car garage sits and where I assume he parked his patrol car so it wouldn't be seen.

I head back inside, lock the door and set the alarm system. The exterior cameras recorded that entire exchange, not that I think it provides any proof of anything against Rafferty. I'm sure if this devolves, he'll deny knowing these men and they'll be ghosts in the wind. Criminals know a thing or two about loyalty as well.

Taking the shotgun and my pistol, I bypass returning them to the gun safe but rather carry them upstairs after collecting my water and peanuts.

Until this mess is resolved, the weapons will remain in proximity to me.

CHAPTER 15

Kat

THE MARDRAGGON JET we're taking to France is ridiculously sumptuous. My family has a jet too, but it's small and meant to fly shorter distances. We use it mainly to travel to shows around the United States while our horses are transported by haulers.

But this jet... wow! The cabin is segmented into multiple zones to include a lounge area, dining/meeting space, and a private rest area toward the back. In between the cabin and the cockpit is a galley where a flight attendant is able to prepare almost any type of food or drink we might want during our trip across the Atlantic.

The central feature is a luxurious seating arrangement configured for both relaxation and dining. On each side of the plane, there's a polished retractable wooden table with two plush chairs on each side that face one another. The chairs are covered in the softest cream leather I've ever felt and ergonomically designed so I feel like I'm floating. Sylvie had fun playing with all the settings which include warmers, cooling vents and even massage.

The interior is done in all leather, high-end wood trim and chrome. Custom carpeting in navy and gold bearing the family's dragon logo in the center runs the length of the jet. There's a high-definition entertainment system as well as a variety of light settings and individual climate controls, depending on your mood. There's even a sofa that converts into a bed and a full-size bathroom in the back with luxurious toiletries and fluffy towels.

The flight attendant approaches us with a tray expertly balanced in her hand. She sets a Shirley Temple in front of Sylvie, who leans forward for a sip through the thin straw. The attendant is beautiful, early twenties, dressed in a pair of navy palazzo pants and a white blouse with a silk tie around her neck. Her makeup is flawless and I can't help but notice the longing looks she shoots toward Gabe.

He's ignoring her for now, focused on a newspaper he brought to read.

Sylvie fishes into the drink and grabs the cherry floating on top before plopping it in her mouth. The attendant sets a sparkling water in a cut crystal glass before Gabe and then one with a Diet Coke for me.

"Will there be anything else?" she asks, her eyes focused only on Gabe.

"No thank you," he replies, his full attention never leaving whatever story he's reading. She offers me and

Sylvie a bland smile and heads back to the galley.

Gabe's head lifts and he glances at my drink with a teasing smirk. "You know that stuff is crap for your body, right?"

I roll my eyes, picking up the glass and lifting it in a mock toast. "Thank you, Dr. Mardraggon. But I'll take my chances. I was up late last night and need the caffeine."

Something close to worry flickers over his face and he nods toward the couch. "Why don't you take a nap?"

"I think I'd rather suffer," I say with a smile and then turn to Sylvie. "Good drink?"

She shrugs and picks it up, forgoing the tiny straw to take a delicate sip. "Think I can have some more cherries?"

Gabe says yes at the same time I say no.

I pin a hard look at Gabe. "Those are full of sugar and bad for the body."

Gabe inclines his head with a smirk. "Touché."

We've only been in the air for about twenty minutes and Sylvie is finally starting to unwind from the excitement. She's been chattering nonstop about everything she wants to show us in Saint-Émilion, including her friends, her favorite shops and most importantly, the château and winery. She's a child who had utter freedom inside an idyllic lifestyle. She was a girl who ran among the vineyards with her dog on her heels and while I know her life with us will be just as amazing, I find myself drawn to the magic of Sylvie's enthusiasm.

It makes me immensely grateful that Ethan decided to let her do this. I'm also grateful that my brothers agreed to take over my duties, enabling me to take this trip. Granted, they still grumbled about what an asshole Gabe is every time I ran into them the last few days. But nothing can dampen my anticipation of seeing France for the first time.

"I think I'm going to watch a movie," Sylvie announces and then reaches over to her backpack. Pulling out an iPad and a set of headphones, I watch as she puts on *The Hunger Games*. She's read the books and is now completely obsessed with the movies, having watched them all more than once.

Gabe and I share a smile, a silent agreement of our mutual happiness for this experience for Sylvie. It's a rare moment of connection and one that does not go unnoticed over how good that makes me feel. I know I should feel guilty for such thoughts, or perhaps I should be chastising myself for getting drawn back to this man in a personal way. But the truth is Gabe and I have rekindled a personal connection that transcends the feud and even our bitter breakup. Sylvie's obviously the catalyst and I have no choice but to see where this goes.

"Are you interested in going over the schedule of events?" Gabe asks.

I blink at him, a little confused, but then I realize he's talking about all the things we have to accomplish on this trip.

"Sure," I reply easily.

"Why don't you come sit on this side," he says, pulling his laptop out of a leather satchel. "That way you can see my computer."

Sylvie doesn't even look up from her movie as I undo my seat belt. Gabe slides over to the chair closest to the window and fires up his laptop as I take the seat next to him. The smell of his cologne is a little too tantalizing and evokes strong memories of our times together. He still wears the same scent, something I noticed when I fell off Shadow and found him hovering over me in the barn.

"You need to buckle up," he says, and before I can even think to slap his hands away, he's fastening my belt.

He's so nonchalant about it while my pulse races, but then he's pulling up his calendar and launches into what we have planned for each day, including a tour of the winery and vineyards with Esteban, the general manager. We will also be tasting the various products and meet with the potential investors Gabe has lined up, an impressive feat since this trip was so spur of the moment. Apparently, though, Alaine had been working on this for the last year before her death.

The day after this investor meeting is most important as we'll be sitting down with the winery's board of directors to discuss the plans for expansion. They apparently have a big presentation for us to consider and depending on how the investors shake out, it could be something we need to move on quickly.

Of course, none of this is my call but rather will be a joint decision for Ethan and Gabe to make for Sylvie's benefit, but my brother is depending on me to analyze this carefully to determine if it's something he can do. He told me the other day that he'll trust my judgment on this and I almost puked from the added responsibility.

It's funny, though. I've decided that I'll have to lean on Gabe's business savvy to make any decisions, and it has never once crossed my mind that I shouldn't trust him where the business is concerned. It appears that even though he's a Mardraggon and he's hurt me in the past, it hasn't turned me against him completely.

Gabe's interrupted by a phone call and I'm startled that he actually gets cell coverage at thirty thousand feet. I presume that's one of the benefits of flying privately. I try not to eavesdrop but he doesn't make any effort to hide his conversation as I'm sitting right beside him. I surf my phone, which is connected to the plane's Wi-Fi, but as I listen, it doesn't take me long to realize the call has something to do with his capacity as the head of Mardraggon Enterprises. There's a lot of high-level talk that I don't understand, once again reiterating my lack of business experience and the mounting pressure upon me to make sure I understand things. Regardless, it's fascinating… and admittedly a little sexy to see him in his element.

His tone is decidedly formal, each word reflecting the weight of the decisions on his shoulders. "We need a thorough analysis of the current tariff impacts and potential market disruptions in the next quarter. It's imperative we align our production forecasts accordingly," he states, his voice a mixture of command and contemplation. "Also, let's expedite the review of our aging inventory. Optimal turnover is crucial, especially with the upcoming summer demands. Ensure that the finance team prepares a detailed forecast by next week."

Gabe pauses, listening intently as his gaze focuses out the window. "Regarding the partnership with the UK distributors, ensure all contractual agreements are vetted for compliance with both our standards and local regulations. We can't afford to overlook anything there. And yes, please schedule a follow-up with the branding team. It's time we pushed forward with the new marketing strategies we discussed."

My head spins at how he keeps all of this straight. Gabe's voice fades slightly as he shifts topics. "Lastly, update me tomorrow on the status of the water sourcing issue. I want that resolved before it affects production. Keep me in the loop with any developments."

When Gabe hangs up, he looks at me with apology. "Sorry about that. I'm going to have to conduct some Mardraggon business here and there while we're on this trip."

"So… chairman of the board now, huh?" I try to sound casual. "You've kind of been thrown into the deep end, especially considering why you had to take over."

Gabe's eyes glitter with confidence. "Make no doubt, I ousted my father because that was what was best for the company, but I'm not thrashing around in the deep end. I know exactly what I'm doing."

I have no doubt he means that, but I am curious. "No regrets about removing Lionel from the board?"

"It had to be done, Kat. I had to protect the company."

"Just like you had to protect Sylvie," I murmur, a flush of gratitude surging through me at the reminder of how Gabe's life has changed in many ways because of what his father did. But one way that's rarely acknowledged is that Gabe was a hero when it mattered.

I'm surprised when he turns the table on me and asks, "And you? How are you handling everything on your plate? I know you have your own duties at the farm, but taking on the winery business with me has got to be stretching you thin."

I exhale, his question causing the weight to feel a tiny bit heavier. "It's never-ending. And in addition to my regular job and the winery, I'm also handling all the medical oversight for the horses. Everyone in the family has pulled something off Ethan's shoulders to give him breathing room. It's like juggling knives."

Gabe chuckles and with a look of genuine interest on his face says, "I'm not sure I really understand everything that you or your family does. Educate me."

"Yeah, I guess we never talked about that stuff back when we were together." The words come out of my mouth unbidden and for a fearful moment, I'm concerned that Sylvie heard that. My gaze snaps to her but she's engrossed in her movie. I move far away from that subject and launch into answering his question. "Blackburn Farms is the largest breeding and training facility for American saddlebreds in the country."

Gabe's eyes flare in surprise and I'm honestly confused how he doesn't know that. We have business interests in the same small slice of Shelby County, but I guess when you mutually hate one another for decades upon decades, families don't tend to get into the important details.

"We have over a thousand acres of land, two hundred brood mares, almost seventy retired horses, nine studs and plenty of foals and yearlings that rotate through. I have no clue how many staff total and it fluctuates seasonally, but I'd guess we average anywhere from fifty to seventy-five people at a time."

"Doing what?" he asks.

"Stable workers, grooms, trainers, veterinarians, administrative staff, maintenance techs. That's just off the top of my head."

Gabe issues a low whistle. "Impressive. I wish I'd asked more about it before."

I'm uncomfortable that he's bringing up our past, especially with Sylvie sitting beside us and the chance that the conversation could turn volatile. I shift attention back to him, delving into something that's been on my mind. "Tell me more about Alaine. What was she like?"

I've heard Sylvie talk about her mother on many occasions because it's a subject everyone in my family encourages. None of us forget that only a few short months ago, Sylvie lost her mother to cancer and then was thrust into an alien world. So we push to keep that connection alive, which is also why Ethan allowed her to come to France with Gabe.

Expression softening, Gabe taps his finger against his glass as he ponders. "I don't quite know how to describe my sister. She was incredible, the best mom to Sylvie. She was so passionate about everything she did, especially the vineyard. That made her a formidable businesswoman and yet... she was really down-to-earth. Nothing like me or my parents in that respect, but I expect that's because she got away from them as soon as she could."

I don't point out there was a time when I found

Gabe to be genuine and down-to-earth but instead say, "I can tell you were very close to her just by the tone of your voice."

Gabe settles back in his chair and nods. "We only had each other. Our parents weren't very… well, parental. I guess it's okay for me to say it out loud now given everything that's happened the last few weeks, but they're both cold. Detached. Alaine and I were raised by a rotating door of nannies. So yeah… we only had each other." His gaze shifts over to Sylvie. "And now she's all I've got."

Understanding dawns on me. Sylvie isn't just his niece, she's his last connection to his sister. The only part of his family that was genuine and loving. The only part of his family that would speak to his own humanity.

Gabe clears his throat and rises from his seat. He's dressed casually in a pair of khaki pants and a black polo shirt with the Mardraggon Bourbon logo of a flying golden dragon over the left breast. "Excuse me a moment… I need to check on something." He moves to the back of the plane, pulling his phone out of his pocket. He puts it to his ear, connecting a call.

I know he would like me to believe that he has business to attend to, but I can tell that he was feeling emotional in remembering his sister. I don't begrudge him that vulnerability and God help me, it makes him more attractive. It reminds me of the man I knew long ago, the one I lost my heart to.

CHAPTER 16

Kat

W HEN I THINK of growing up in Kentucky, especially the feud between the Blackburns and the Mardraggons, I often get a sense of awe over how long ago it started. Over a hundred and seventy years— that span used to seem unfathomable to me. But as I walk the ancient streets of Saint-Émilion, I realize our American feud happened the equivalent of a yesterday to the French.

I can understand why Sylvie is so homesick for this picturesque town in the Bordeaux region. The town was formed in the eighth century—over a thousand years ago—and while math has never been my forte, those numbers make my head spin. I've been absolutely charmed by the stone architecture and the narrow cobblestone streets. Because the town sits atop a hill, stunning views of the vineyards stretch as far as the eye can see, the Dordogne River meandering in the distance.

I've walked the streets early in the morning each day

we've been here, feeling more confident in myself to bridge the language barrier by lucking into residents who speak English or miming what I need when inside a bakery or coffee shop.

Gabe has taken to working on Mardraggon business first thing in the morning and I've used the time to explore. Sylvie has been the social butterfly, visiting dear friends she was forced to leave behind without proper goodbyes. While I wanted her by my side as I experienced my first trip to Europe, I also could never deny her the opportunity to soak up every bit of homecoming that she could. She stayed at a friend's house yesterday and last night.

Glancing at my watch, I see it's nearing nine a.m. and I have to be back at the château in about an hour to meet Gabe. We're going to review the notes from our meetings regarding the expansion as well as the portfolios of interested investors.

My stomach rumbles, the perfect invitation to stop inside my new favorite boulangerie on the Place du Marché where I've taken to eating baguette slices with butter and jam. Nothing has ever tasted as good, especially sitting outside at their little wrought iron tables while inhaling the scent of grape leaves in the air from all the vineyards surrounding the town.

I get my food along with a strong cup of coffee and settle into a table that allows me to see the bell tower of the Saint-Émilion Monolithic Church. I toured it our first full day here when we let Sylvie be our guide. It's an architectural wonder, partially carved from a single block of limestone for which the region is known. We climbed to the top of the bell tower and my breath was robbed upon taking in the panoramic view of the region. From high above, the vineyards were segregated into asymmetrical blocks of different varieties of grapes, creating a patchwork quilt of color.

Keeping one eye on my watch, since it's a good twenty-minute walk to the château, I let my attention follow the people milling around. Many are tourists but some are locals, and it's not hard to tell the difference.

I'm slathering orange marmalade onto another baguette slice when a shadow falls over my table. I look up to see Gabe standing there, casual in a pair of jeans and a button-down shirt. He settles into the chair opposite me and without asking takes the baguette from my hand. "I'm starving. I haven't had a chance to eat breakfast."

"Hey," I exclaim, only slightly irritated, and it fizzles just as quickly when he winks at me before taking a bite. "What are you doing here?"

"It was too nice a morning to keep working, so I canceled a meeting and decided to come find you. Figured we could talk business while we walk around and look at cool old stuff."

I finish the last bit of my coffee, loving the bitter bite

after the sweetness of the marmalade. He notes the skeptical look on my face.

"What?" he inquires. "I know how to have fun."

This is laughable as Gabe has done nothing but work, other than that first day we hung out with Sylvie. Granted, I've worked too, focusing on administrative stuff I could handle with the convenience of a good Wi-Fi connection at the château, but Gabe is hard-core devoted. He reminds me so much of Ethan, managing an empire and making it look easy, even though we all know it's not.

"If you say so," I mutter.

Gabe pops the last piece of bread into his mouth and brushes off his hands. He chews, swallows, and then rises from the chair. "Come on. Let's take a walk."

We meander through the town and back down a winding lane toward the château, which sits right in the middle of vine plots. The winery grows mainly two types of grapes, making their signature blend from merlot and cabernet franc varieties. I learned during our tour of the winery—which included a tasting—that the merlot grape lends flavors of plum and black cherry to the wine, and the cabernet franc offers a spicy bouquet that hints at tobacco and raspberry.

I tried my hardest to taste those things within the rich, red wine, but my palate is apparently not very sophisticated. All I know is that the wine tasted good and that was the extent of my input into the product. Gabe thought it hilarious when I later confided to him that I had no ability to taste any of that stuff.

"You'll have to come do a bourbon tasting with me. I can coach you through how to taste certain qualities. It takes practice."

I didn't respond because that sounds like something lovers might do together, or even friends.

We're not even friends.

We reach the château built in the same golden-yellow limestone that most buildings here have been done in. It can seem dull at times, especially in the town limits where all the buildings are the same color, but there's something to be said about the way the structures glow warmly during sunset, taking on a rich, amber hue from the sun's dying rays.

Very similar to Gabe's eyes when he's feeling extreme emotion.

The château itself is a home little girls' dreams are made of and while I love our historical house back in Kentucky, I can see why Sylvie misses this place so much. The massive three-story structure has steeply pitched roofs covered in slate tiles and on the front corners are two elegant towers with conical roofs. I can almost imagine the prince climbing up to kiss the princess, and from the windows in those rooms—one a library and the other a bedroom—the view of the vineyards is beyond compare.

The château is set on expansive grounds with meticulously maintained gardens that bloom with a variety of flowers and shrubs. Sylvie told us that gardening was her mother's hobby and someone has been doing a beautiful job in caring for the plants in her absence.

The backyard slopes downward, flanked by rows of ancient cedar trees. The vineyards stretch out beyond with rows of grapevines meticulously tended, following the gentle roll of the hills.

It's toward the rows of grapes that we walk, chatting about the expansion. Gabe does most of the talking while I listen.

"We need to be aggressive but practical." Gabe reaches out, plucks a small grape—no bigger than the size of a pea at this point in the season—off a merlot bunch and examines it. The end of each row has a post with a plaque identifying the grape variety, which is the only way I know it's a merlot. "We can't afford a misstep on this expansion, especially since you and I are out of our element."

I shake my head. "I'm out of my element. This is your forte."

"Bourbon isn't the same as wine, not to mention, this is a French company and product. Trust me, I'm out of my element."

I glance over at him, the morning sun making his

blond hair glow like a halo but I know he's no angel. "You don't ever act like it. You're always so in control."

"Only because I work hard at looking like I'm in control," he replies, and while he sounds like he's jesting, I get the feeling he's serious. "We can't just throw money at this idea, even if we have legit investors. We need a sustainable approach. This is going to be a long and costly process, results not being seen until probably at least ten years down the road. I have my own business to run, and you're busy as hell."

"It sounds daunting. What am I supposed to tell Ethan when I barely understand this stuff?"

"I don't think Ethan is looking for a recommendation from you as to the viability of these suggested plans. I think he's looking for you to gut check yourself as far as I'm concerned."

"I'm not following you," I say hesitantly, although I think I've got an inkling as to what he means.

Gabe stops, turns to face me. "Your brother is smart. He's a businessman, same as me. He can have any number of advisors evaluate all this stuff and tell him what to do, but he's letting you handle this for one reason only."

"And that is?"

"To find out if your family can trust me."

I stare at Gabe because I used to trust him and then he betrayed me. Abandoned me. The easy answer to my brother should be *"No, we can't trust Gabe Mardraggon."*

But he's not the same man I knew. He's become a protector to Sylvie, turned his back on his father and that familial legacy, and he's a man who loves his niece so thoroughly, I'm not sure there's anything he wouldn't do for her.

That all has to go into this gut check that Gabe is talking about. I have to reconcile my past feelings and experiences with the man standing before me now. But to admit that I think it's okay to trust Gabe as it involves Sylvie and the winery means I might have to admit he's changed for the better. It might mean there's room to forgive and perhaps evaluate that kiss we had, and what seems to be a growing connection and I'm not sure I can do that.

"I don't know," I say, crossing my arms over my stomach. I look off into the distance over the fertile green hills. "Maybe we should just let the winery run as is for a while. It's making a good profit and the oversight is manageable."

Gabe stares at me, his expression teetering somewhere between admiration and annoyance. "When did you become so cautious? I remember a girl who used to take risks, who wasn't afraid to chase what she wanted."

"A lot has changed since then," I reply, my arms shifting to cross over my chest. Defiance rather than self-protection. "I had to grow up and I don't call that being cautious. I call that being wise."

The big jerk isn't chastened by my veiled reference to the reasons I had to grow up—mainly his lack of devotion to me. His eyes roam the length of my body and in a husky, sexually taunting voice, he says, "Yes, you have grown up, and very nicely indeed."

"Oh, shut up," I growl and backhand him lightly in the chest. There's no heat in my strike because it's all centered in my lower belly where his words have a very unwanted effect on me.

Gabe moves lightning fast, catching my wrist. But he doesn't push me away, rather reels me in slowly until our hands are trapped between our bodies.

The air thickens, charged with the history and tension of what was left unsaid all those years ago. "Why do you think we keep circling back to each other?"

"Because I'm a glutton for punishment," I bite out.

His voice is low, rumbling. "Oh, I think it's more than that."

My breath hitches and my legs wobble. "It's bad history. That's all."

"Or a new future," he counters softly, and all my fears—or are they dreams—come true as his mouth descends onto mine.

It's not that fiery crash of lips on the night of the gala but something so terrifyingly sweet, I almost believe I could forgive Gabe for breaking my heart. His mouth roams mine, a slight brush of tongues, a gentle exploration, as if he's trying to lay down new memories to block out the old.

A rebranding of sorts.

As quickly as it starts, it ends, with Gabe being the one who pulls back to peer down at me. I can't read his expression, but I expect that's intentional as he's trying to read mine without providing any influence.

He's using silence to force me to say if this is okay.

Continue? Slap him? Tell him to go to hell? Ask him to kiss me again.

"Aunt Kat," Sylvie calls in the distance. I try to jerk away, but Gabe holds my hand tight for a second. My head twists and I see her making her way to the cedars where her complete view of us is momentarily obstructed.

Did she see that kiss or was she too far away?

I look back to Gabe, still holding tight to my hand. I stare at him imploringly to let me go before Sylvie can see us in this intimate position.

"We need to talk," he says.

"We talk all the time," I mutter.

"About us."

"There is no us," I snap and jerk hard, my hand sliding free as I step back.

"There could be, Kat. Second chances happen all the time."

196

"Aunt Kat. Uncle Gabe," Sylvie calls again and I see her waving at us enthusiastically as she clears the cedars and lopes down a gentle incline to reach us. By the tone of her voice, I can tell she didn't see anything.

"Kat," Gabe says softly, and I look back at him. His eyes are the ones beseeching now. "Can we talk?"

The thud of Sylvie's feet on the earth has me distracted so I mutter, "Maybe," and then turn back to her.

"Hey, kiddo," I say, opening my arms for a hug. She flies into them and I embrace her tight. "Have a good time at Camille's?"

Camille was a classmate of Sylvie's and the closest friend she left behind. This is the second night she stayed over with her.

"Oui," she says with a toothy grin. "Nous nous sommes tellement amusées!"

I laugh because since returning to her homeland, Sylvie has slipped back into French as if it's a natural extension of her body, like her arm or leg. "English, please!"

"We had so much fun," she corrects and then slips from my arms to hug Gabe. "Her parents took us kayaking yesterday afternoon on the Dordogne and then we had a bonfire in their yard last night. Her dad told us ghost stories, but we weren't afraid." She then glances back to me, her expression chagrined. "Much."

Tonight, Sylvie is going to another overnighter with

a group of girls who she took ballet with for several years and while she hasn't shown any interest in returning to dance in Kentucky, her bonds with these young girls are strong. One of the mothers suggested a big sleepover at their house and though it's our last night in France, I can't deny her the opportunity to squeeze every drop out of this visit.

"What do you want to do for the day?" I ask as she steps back from Gabe and leans over to look at a bunch of grapes. She doesn't pick one the way Gabe did but turns a full bunch in her hands. This is the stage known as fruit set, something I learned this week, and the tiny green spheres haven't accumulated any significant sugar. They're still green to match the color of the leaves but by early September, they'll be ready for harvest.

It's astounding to me that this little girl, only ten years old, examines these grapes with the seasoned eye of a master vintner. She may be a Blackburn now and she's being raised on a horse farm in Kentucky but I'm seeing her future, and I know it's going to be here.

"We can do whatever you want until it's time for your sleepover," I say, my gaze landing on Gabe. I know that I can't let the overwhelming nature of this winery let me be complacent when it comes to making sure we preserve Sylvie's legacy. I can help Gabe make this place even better. "And maybe tonight we can work on a game plan for the expansion."

Gabe nods, his mouth curving into a pleasing smile.

For a moment, I only focus on that mouth, remembering the whisper-soft kiss we just shared, and I wonder if something has actually reignited between us. It was an impulsive act but it doesn't mean it lacked meaning or merit.

I just have to figure out if I want to explore this further and if so, how will I navigate the host of problems it will create, given our bitter past and the fact our families don't trust each other?

CHAPTER 17

Gabe

WHEN KAT AND I arrive back at the château, it's almost eleven p.m. I'm feeling the length of the day within the yawn I'm suppressing, but Kat doesn't hold hers back. Our flight leaves tomorrow morning and we still have to pack.

After Sylvie found us in the vineyard this morning, we ended up taking her to the nearby town of Libourne, which is only about nine kilometers away. It sits at the confluence of the Isle and Dordogne Rivers and is famous for its vibrant market held in the Place Abel Surchamp at the center of town. It's one of the largest in the region and offers a huge range of local products, including fresh produce, wines, cheeses and other regional specialties. We wandered through the market, hit a few museums, and I ended up buying a portrait that caught Sylvie's eye in an art gallery. It was of the valley just outside of Saint-Émilion and while she didn't ask for it, I could see it touched her because it is a perfect rendition of her homeland and everything she misses. After she and Kat wandered off, I met with the gallery director and arranged for payment and shipping.

We then dropped Sylvie off for her sleepover and I talked Kat into joining me for dinner at a well-hidden bistro Esteban recommended. We dined on fresh oysters from the Bay of Biscay, lamb cooked in a rich sauce made with a local red wine produced at a neighboring vineyard, sea bass with lemon and capers, and we finished it all off with a shared strawberry tart. The meal was extravagant but on the lighter side. We spent the entire time talking business, although I would have preferred to talk about the kiss we shared before Sylvie came upon us.

For some reason, Kat seems to have a renewed vigor and enthusiasm about expanding the winery. I'm not sure what clicked with her, but she seems hell-bent on being able to go to Ethan with a recommendation that we move forward.

I obviously want to move forward and I've got my people back in Kentucky checking out the investors. But if everything falls into place as I expect, we could begin true efforts to expand the winery according to Alaine's vision and make a beautiful legacy for Sylvie to return to when she wants.

And there's no doubt in my mind this child will return here. While she has learned to gain happiness with her new family and has undoubtedly formed deeply poignant bonds with Ethan, Kat and the other members, Sylvie is French through and through. She might even go to college in the States, but afterward I know without a doubt she's going to come back one day and run this winery.

As someone who heads an empire based on something similar, nothing would make me prouder.

"I'm exhausted," Kat says with another yawn. "And I haven't even thought about packing."

"We've got time in the morning." The benefit of having our own plane means we can leave whenever we want and we're not scheduled to take off until ten a.m.

"I know," Kat says with a chuckle. She heads for the staircase that leads up to the second floor of guest suites. "But I've got to get Sylvie packed up too. I peeked into her room today and it looks like a bomb exploded in there. I think I'm going to do that tonight."

She makes it halfway up the staircase before I call her name. "Kat."

With one hand on the banister, she glances back at me with a raised eyebrow.

"Are we going to talk about the kiss?"

Her expression shutters and I can't read a damn thing on her face. "I don't think that's a good idea."

"Because you're afraid to start something with me?"

"Yes."

She doesn't say anything else. She just laid it bare that she's afraid and I can't alleviate that for her.

"I can't promise I won't hurt you again," I say to her, moving toward the staircase but not ascending, merely looking up at her. "I can't say that not because it isn't true, but because you wouldn't trust it."

She nods, rubbing the back of her neck. "I find things very confusing with you. I'm trying to reconcile an abrupt change of feelings where you're concerned. I think us being intimate would only confuse things more for me."

That's disappointing to hear. I had hoped she might be willing to take a chance, but because I hurt her so badly before and because I have been working so hard to gain not only her trust but the Blackburns' trust in general, I don't push.

I simply nod. "I understand."

Kat bestows on me what I think is her first genuine smile since we reconnected. "Thanks for understanding and thank you again for a great dinner tonight."

"You're very welcome."

Kat resumes her trek up the stairs but I call her name one more time. "Kat."

When she looks back at me, I ask, "Do you think we can have a friendship?"

"I think we already do."

Christ, my heart swells with pure joy. "That's good."

"Good night, Gabe."

"Good night, Hell Kat." She rolls her eyes at me and then disappears up the staircase and to the left to her guest bedroom.

When I hear her door close, I make my own way up, working at the buttons on my sleeves. By the time I make it to my room, which is right off the top landing, I'm removing my shirt. I have no qualms about tossing it on the floor near my suitcase as I'll have to get packed eventually. But I'm exhausted too and I'm tired of spending so much of my thought energy on Kat. I'm eager to fall into dreamless sleep, if I can be so lucky.

My hands go to my belt to undo it but still when there's a faint knock on my door. Pulse skittering—it can only be Kat since we're the only two in the house—I walk that way. Glancing at my shirt not five feet away on the floor, I consider putting it back on, but Kat has seen all of me and I'm not modest.

I open the door to find her there, head looking off down the hall from where she came, fingers twisted in what could be taken as anxiousness.

"Are you okay?" I ask.

Her head whips my way—roaming my chest before locking with my eyes. And she's brutally honest. "No, I'm not."

Thoughts are immediately on Sylvie and the winery. I go into protective mode, my hands going to hers.

"Whatever it is, it'll be fine. I can handle all of this for Sylvie—"

Kat shakes her head, that glorious black hair falling around her shoulders. "It's not Sylvie. It's that kiss. Or rather, those kisses. At the gala, and then this morning."

"Oh," I exhale harshly, thrilled she wants to talk about it rather than sweep it under the rug the way she's been doing.

Years have passed since our very first kiss in college, years filled with memories that lingered like the faint trace of a once-familiar perfume. Now, standing close to her like this, the weight of everything unsaid charging the air, I know we're on the brink of something big.

My eyes search hers, taking in the green pools of indecision, frustration and yearning. Every emotion that's had my gut tied in knots. The vulnerability in her gaze echoes how I feel, and I'm not afraid to show it.

I can't be, not when she sought me out.

Kat bites her lip, a nervous movement I remember all too well. I also remember wanting to protect her and quell that anxiety whenever I saw it, from that day years ago where I saw how troubled she was by the daunting equations of that college math class.

Slowly, I brush a stray lock of hair from her face. The touch is familiar and thrilling, a reminder of what had been and what could still be if Kat would open up. She closes her eyes at my touch, a soft sigh escaping her as she leans into my palm. My heart trips at what might be a slip of resistance.

The moment stretches, taut with anticipation, until finally I can't take it anymore. My head bends and my lips graze against hers tenderly while her eyes are still closed. Her body jerks slightly but she sighs as if she's in a very good dream.

I'm gentle to start, taking my time to relearn the map of her lips and tongue, but it's Kat's hands going to the back of my neck and the pressure she puts there that tells me she wants more. The kiss deepens and I'm tight as a bowstring as our hesitation seems to melt away.

I've never stopped wanting this woman, even when we hated each other.

Even when we moved on.

Driven now by a previously unrealized pent-up longing, I pull her hard against me and smile at her gasp of surprise. But then she's kissing me back and we quickly slide out of control, spiraling into each other. With a hand threading through her hair, I grip tightly and gently pull her away.

Those green eyes flutter open, sparking with lust, and I groan because it makes it even harder to say what I'm about to say. "We're getting ready to cross a line, Kat. If I start touching you, I won't stop."

I've got one hand at the back of her head, the other at her hip, and yet I feel a full-body shudder ripple through her.

Eyes locked onto mine, she says, "I wonder how your touch would feel after all these years? Where might your hands wander? Would you be sure and confident, or hesitant because we've both changed?" She tilts her head, brushes her lips along my neck and now I'm the one shuddering. Her voice goes husky and promising. "I wonder if you'd lose control…"

"Jesus Christ, Hell Kat," I mutter, leaning in and brushing my nose along hers. "Are you trying to get yourself fucked?"

Eyes still clouded with passion, a certain clarity filters in and her tone is deadly calm. "Would it be wrong?"

I shake my head. "Not in any way."

She considers that a long moment.

Some would say way too long, but then I see resolve in that ferny stare. She rises up to kiss me again, but I hold her in check. Her brows furrow in confusion.

"I want you to say the words, Kat."

Her eyes narrow. "The words?"

"I want you to ask for it. I want to know that you want this."

Eyes hooded, glittering with challenge, Kat once again rises up and puts her mouth on mine, not to kiss me but to bite my bottom lip. She's not gentle but makes sure to lick the sting away.

A rumble of disapproval that she's being impish

emanates in a growl. "Christ, you're a piece of work."

A complaint to be sure, but not in any meaningful way that would stop what I'm about to do. My lips crash onto hers as I lift her up, my hands under her ass. I turn, walk her into my room and we tumble onto the bed.

Kat has never been wishy-washy and when she commits, she's normally all in. But in the off chance she gets inside her head and decides this is wrong, I start to touch her in all the forbidden places. My hand squeezes her breast before my palm presses between her legs, feeling heat through the denim.

I hiss in surprise and pleasure when she grips my hardening length, then curse when she squeezes me. She's a wildcat right now, but then again, she always was. Wild, uninhibited, so fucking sure of her sensuality.

"Too many clothes," she gasps, hands going to my belt buckle.

Chuckling, I bat her hands away. "I've already got a head start. Let's work on you."

I had every intention of stripping her slowly, taking my time with every inch revealed. I want to drag this out so it never ends but Kat and I have never really been slow with things. Almost with an animalistic urgency, we tear at each other's clothes, trying to force material away from bare skin and then finally... finally, we're naked and wrapped up with each other in the middle of the mattress.

It's not until this moment that I realize, I want Kat in all ways. Not just in this bed, our bodies entwined. I want her heart again. I want a future with her, just the way I'd envisioned but didn't have the maturity or the confidence to act on.

I'm not the same man I was all those years ago. I've changed over time, and in the last two months, I've changed even more. I'm confident I can be the type of man Kat needs me to be, but she's going to be a tough nut to crack. I have no doubt she's got her heart wrapped up tight in a protective layer of Gabe-resistant armor.

I may have been that way once, but the man I am now is not afraid of a challenge. In fact, I kind of relish it.

CHAPTER 18

Kat

M Y HEART IS slamming so hard in my chest, I'm afraid my ribs might break. I've never been with a man like Gabe in the years since we broke up, and this older, sexier and more mature Gabe is a thousand times more potent.

He kisses me… so damn domineering, and I feel it down to the marrow in my bones. His mouth devours mine, his hands possessively roaming. Within every touch, I can read his thoughts.

This is mine.

And this is mine.

I'll take that too.

Gabe was ever the alpha and it turned me on back then. Still does for that matter, but I have to keep in mind, I'm only willing to let him possess my body right now. If he tries to go alpha on anything else, I'll shut it down.

Lifting his head, he stares at me, a perplexed expression on his face. "What's wrong?"

"What do you mean?" I counter, stroking his bare chest. "Shut up and kiss me."

My hand goes to the back of his neck to pull him down but he's too strong and holds himself above me. "You may think otherwise, but I still read Kat Blackburn just fine. Your body tensed up, and not in the way it normally does when I'm touching you."

I roll my eyes. "Get over yourself, Gabe. I'm perfectly fine and would like to resume what we were doing."

He ignores me. "Because if you're having feelings you want to talk about—"

"I want to have sex, Gabe. If you think I'm worried about having my heart broken again, you can rest assured, that's not a worry at all because that would be an impossible task. Now… do you want to kiss me or do you want me to go back to my room?"

Gabe stares at me a long, hard moment and I think he might just kick me out of his bed, but then his lips arc into a sly smile. "I'd much rather have sex than talk feelings."

"Then let's get on with it," I say tartly.

He chuckles as he bends down to kiss me again, his humor vibrating through me. I'm smiling as I accept his tongue into my mouth, my fingers sliding into his soft hair.

Once again, his hands are all over me and I react no differently from how I did when we were together in college.

Swiftly, achingly. "More," I demand in between hot kisses and urgent strokes over my breasts, between my legs.

Gabe is so masterful in his ministrations, and I'm so keenly attuned to every touch and whisper that within a matter of moments, I'm a writhing mess of need. His hand between my legs explores, his fingers probing and finding me wet and ready for him. I'd gladly take a quick, hard tumble with the man and I'm not above begging to get what I want.

I leave the words though and try with actions, spreading my legs farther and using my hands at his back to urge him onto me. Gabe doesn't move, holding rock solid above me as he kisses and touches. With my hand, I palm the swell of his erection and although he groans and bucks, he doesn't do more than that.

Instead, he squeezes my breast, plucks at my nipple, making them feel heavy with need. But he abandons my breasts to stroke over my stomach, then back down between my legs, right over my clit until my hips buck and the words I thought I could keep at bay tumble out. "Please, Gabe. For the love of your fine bourbon, will you just fuck me."

"That's my Kat." He laughs huskily. "Always so demanding."

I want to say *not your Kat*, but a spasm knocks the words back down my throat as the pad of his finger rubs along my sex before sinking deep into me. I groan, my back arching and my eyes squeezing tight to shut out all other distractions. I just want to feel.

"Oh, Kat," Gabe murmurs, his lips at my throat. "I've hardly touched you and you're so wet for me."

Damn him to hell, but his words are as much a turn-on as anything. His foreplay masterful, my hips rotate as if they have a mind of their own. It embarrasses me how well he can play my body, and I can't help but try to put him in his place. "I was thinking about someone else," I grit out.

He doesn't reply but I feel that finger moving in and out of me. My eyes open with curiosity and I find Gabe has angled his body, head bent so he can watch his movements, as if utterly fascinated by something he's never seen. My own gaze travels down my body and I'm enthralled by his big hand moving so assuredly against me. I'm beyond turned on that Gabe seems transfixed by it and a rush of wetness betrays my attempt to be aloof in all of this.

Gabe doesn't look at me but says offhandedly, "Yeah… don't buy you're thinking of anyone else but me and my fingers right now."

I grit my teeth, prepared to blast him, but a slick finger circles my clit and it feels so damn good, I cry out. A pleasured exclamation that has Gabe chuckling at his effect on me.

His touch burns in all the right ways, heat sizzling and sparking. A rushing tide of pleasure starts cresting within me and I'm so close but then his hand is gone.

My head jerks upward and I glare at him, but his mouth is there to kiss away my frustration. "Relax," he murmurs against my lips. "While I'd love to just play with you all night, I really need to be inside you."

I sigh into the kiss, grateful he won't make me wait. While I know that Gabe is very skilled at foreplay and can drag it out, making me peak several times before he'd even think about slaking his own needs, I find that eight years away from this man has created an insane quest for immediate gratification. It's almost as if I need him to knock the edge off so I can have some semblance of myself again.

Gabe pulls all the way free, rolling to the edge of the bed to nab his pants. He fishes out his wallet and from inside, a condom. He grins at me playfully and I give it right back to him. I'm grateful he's as prepared as a Boy Scout.

Straddling my body, Gabe rips the condom foil with his teeth. I take his length in hand, stroke him hard a few times, and he growls low in his throat. Molten eyes pinning me in place, he shoves the condom at me. "Might as well make yourself useful."

I remember this so well from our past. Gabe loved my hands on him in this way, an affirmative action that showed how much I wanted it. The same as years before, my hands shake as I glide the condom on. His head tips back, eyes closed to relish the sensation, and he looks like an absolute god risen before me. I squeeze when I'm done and his head dips, dark golden eyes locking onto mine.

Gabe falls forward, his hands coming to the mattress at my shoulders, and my legs part, knees raised and pressing to his hips. His mouth hovers over mine, eyes still holding me in place. I guide him to me and he slowly enters, an agonizing inch at a time. We stare at each other, both unable to look away as he fills my body, and given the traitorous thump in my chest, I'm guessing a bit of my heart too. I hate myself for it, but it's impossible to disentangle emotion from sex.

Later, I promise myself. I'll harden myself later, but for now, I let myself feel it all.

When Gabe is fully seated, our pelvises flush, he finally kisses me again. He doesn't move, just letting his mouth work against mine.

"Gabe…," I whisper against his lips.

He ignores me, staying perfectly still within my body and kissing me thoroughly.

"Please." I hate begging, but he loves it because I feel his mouth curve into a smile.

Then he moves, and oh wow… this is the thing I'd never forget. That connection, the feel of his body locking with mine as if it was the crucial last piece of a puzzle. His thickness filling me, his slow thrusts causing mad ripples of pleasure to assault my every sense.

I'm overwhelmed, out of control, and I hate it all.

Love it all.

Gabe's hand presses between our bodies, his fingers finding that bundle of nerves that he knows will dismantle every last bit of dominion I have over myself. Tension coils tight, the rubber band pulled taut within me, and I consider holding it back but why bother. He'll get it anyway.

I succumb to Gabe, giving it up to the man I should hate but don't. The explosion of pleasure is violent and destructive, tearing me up from the inside out, and I've never felt anything more amazing in my life. I don't know if it's the deep well of bitter emotions we're trying to wade through or the fact that I once loved this man with all my heart, but my orgasm is so powerful, I'm not sure I'm going to be okay.

I groan through the release, my body locking tight.

"Fuck yes," Gabe mutters, his eyes alight with praise. His hips move faster and he tunnels deeper.

As I start to come down from the pinnacle, I feel my eyes closing. Gabe grabs my jaw with his hand and snarls, "Eyes on me, Hell Kat."

I think to disobey him but curiosity wins out. I want to see if he's going to be as undone as I was.

Teeth gritted, neck muscles straining, Gabe rides me fast and hard. I memorize the planes of his face, the pace of his breath, and with one hard thrust, Gabe's expression twists into a ghastly but beautiful portrait of painful pleasure as he orgasms.

"Katherine." My full name, a graveled prayer falling from his mouth.

A long rush of pent-up breath blows across my face and Gabe lowers his body onto mine, utterly spent. Without thought, only by emotion, I wrap my arms around his lower back, my legs around his thighs. He rests his chin on my shoulder, mouth pressed into my neck as his breathing regulates.

After what seems like forever, Gabe speaks first, although he keeps his head lowered. "Are you filled with regret and recrimination?"

"I'm too blissed out to feel anything negative right now, but give me a moment."

I expect him to laugh but instead, he lifts his head and stares down at me. "This wasn't a onetime-only thing, so if you're going to have regrets, let's hash them out now."

My breath catches when I see how serious he is. This wasn't about scratching an itch or giving into some type of hate fuck. Gabe wants to continue, and I had not considered that when I gave in to him tonight.

"I don't have regrets," I say carefully. "But I don't

know what this is."

"I don't either. I just know it's not over."

Something inside of me thrills at the confidence he's exhibiting, but at the same time, I can feel the barriers rising up around me. "We're over. Have been for years."

The corner of his mouth twitches, his eyes twinkling. "We're starting new then."

I shake my head, but his hand grips my jaw again. "Don't deny it. You know there's still something here between us, and if we can get past the hurt…" I try to talk but he amends the path he was taking. "If you can forgive me for what I did to you, then we could build something good, Kat."

Forgive him? Is that what he's seeking?

And he wants to build something new?

"I don't think I can trust you," I say, all the old hurt welling up.

"Let me try at least," he says, his tone slightly pleading, which is something Gabe Mardraggon would never do. "Just… let's keep seeing each other, okay?"

"For sex?"

"Well, yes, for sex. Wasn't that fucking fantastic?" Yeah, it was. The best ever if I'm honest. "But let's continue to rebuild our friendship. We have Sylvie to worry about and it's in her best interests if we all get along."

"That's convenient," I mutter.

"I'm being serious," he growls, pressing his lips down hard on mine. When he lifts, he says, "Please… promise me we can see each other."

I'm not opposed to what we just did. He's right… fucking fantastic. I could do that over and over again with Gabe, but I'm not letting this get any deeper than sex.

"Okay," I say, and I feel his body relax. I shut that down fast. "But we can't tell anyone."

Gabe's eyes narrow. "Keep it a secret."

"Just like back in college," I affirm.

"But you didn't want to keep it a secret."

"I do now."

He studies me thoughtfully and I know he thinks I'm doing this to get back at him. But I'm doing this for self-preservation. If I can keep what Gabe and I have in a bubble, I can prevent feelings from developing. I can keep things contained and under control.

It's my best chance of protecting my heart but deep in my gut I know it's a risk that I could be destroyed, no matter if we keep it to ourselves or tell the world.

"Fine," he finally relents. "We'll keep it a secret."

CHAPTER 19

Gabe

I T WASN'T ONLY but a handful of times I'd sneak onto Blackburn Farms to meet up with Kat at the little apartment above the tack room the summer between our freshman and sophomore years of college. But in those days, Kat would meet me at the farm's boundary where I'd leave my car parked at the edge of an old service road and we'd steal through the night, hand in hand, to our destination. I trusted that everyone who could catch us was tucked away where they should be and there'd be no irate father or brother waiting to lay me low with buckshot.

I don't have those assurances now.

I drove my G 550 because I intend to park on that service road again and my Ferrari sits too low. I intend to sneak along the same paths to that apartment but I don't have the promise of safety. Kat has no idea I'm coming and that's by design. If I'd have asked to come over, I'm quite confident her answer would've been no.

That's not to say she's changed her mind about us continuing to see each other. In fact, she came to my house last night under the guise of working on the winery expansion, but we spent barely thirty seconds talking before we were going at it in my office. Let's just say that my desk got well used and it wasn't to study spreadsheets or investment reports.

We've been back from France for three days now and Kat has played it cool with me. She's not once asked to get together, content to make me work for it.

That's fine as I've got a lot to make up for. But her agreement to spend time with me has been hard to come by and it's hit or miss whether she'll even respond. The reason I'm so sure she would say no if I asked tonight is because last night, after our heart rates had returned to normal and our sweat had cooled, Kat let me pick her up from the desk and carry her up to my bedroom. She then let me take my time with her body, getting reacquainted with all the little sensitive spots that I used to own. She let me put my mouth everywhere and when she climaxed on my tongue, she called out my name with such longing, my chest ached.

And after that was all done, she let me just hold her. Granted, I think she was worn out, a puddle of bliss and quite malleable. I forced her to be vulnerable by holding her tight, talking about inane things. Eventually she relaxed and we managed to have a conversation that had nothing to do with the winery, the original feud or our horrid breakup.

We talked about our trip to France and all the things we did that weren't business related. Charmed by the history, the ancient buildings and the simpler way of life outside the major cities, Kat now yearns to return to Europe and explore. We lay in bed and I told her about my travels, and all I could think was that I'd love to be the one to take her, but to voice that aloud would cause her to shut down and bolt.

So I took what she offered, which was some companionable cuddling and conversation.

Oh, it didn't last long. She eventually realized that we were talking candidly and with ease. If we didn't have a tattered history between us, she might have stayed longer.

But nope. She bolted, and she's been silent this morning. Hasn't responded to my texts, either inviting her to get together or about winery-related items. She's even ignored my text asking how Sylvie has been doing this week since she's attending a horse camp Blackburn Farms is putting on. Sylvie wasn't committed to riding but they do all kinds of fun things on the farm, and her friend Carmen is attending, the main reason she agreed to do it.

Kat has underestimated my determination though, and as I creep stealthily among the quiet and darkened barns, my eyes adjusting to the dark, I don't waste time getting to my destination.

Looking up the staircase that leads to her apartment door, I'm pleased to see her living room light is on and her Jeep is parked beside the building. The sconce light at her door throws a tiny bit of illumination down on me. Everything else around me is dark, including the main house off in the distance on a knoll.

The efficient thing to do would be to march up the stairs and knock on her door.

The smart thing to do would be to call her and let her know I'm here.

If someone were to make a list of my qualities, efficiency and intelligence would be at the top no doubt. But I need to do something different, so I'm going to call on a quality that is rusty at best.

Bending over, I grab some pea gravel and start pelting her window. By about the fifth one, Kat's face appears at the glass and she frowns as she looks out. I can tell when her eyes lock right on me because I can see the flash of irritation from where I'm standing.

She disappears and then the door opens. I drop the gravel, brush my hands off on my jeans and start for the staircase.

"Stop," she says, and I look up to see her holding her palm out to me. "I'm not inviting you in."

"That's good," I say, halting at the bottom step and

leaning my elbow on the railing. "Because I want you to come with me."

"Oh please," she drawls, crossing her arms over her chest. "You came for a booty call but you already had one last night."

I grin up at her. "There's no lie in the fact I'd consider it a perfect evening if I were to end up in your bed, but I really do want you to go somewhere with me."

"Why?" she asks suspiciously.

I throw my arms out and mock her. "Oh come on, Kat. Live a little. Be adventurous. Come with me."

The indecision wars on her face. She's not in her pajamas but I'll bet she wasn't too far off from going to bed as I know she's an early riser. But tonight is too beautiful to let it go to waste.

"Where are we going?" she asks.

"That would be no fun if I told you," I reply, refusing to give her any assurances. She needs to want this or else she'll never get to where I want her to go.

Glancing down at her watch, back inside her apartment, and then back down to her watch, she huffs in frustration. "How long will we be gone?"

"An hour max," I promise.

"Fine," she mutters, grabbing her purse and a jacket. I wait for her to lock up and when she reaches me at the bottom of the stairs, she mutters, "You could have just texted or called rather than sneaking here to throw rocks at my window."

Laughing, I grab her hand to lead her into the darkness and I'm surprised she doesn't pull away. "You haven't responded to any of the texts I've sent today and besides… I thought you would find this charming."

"I find it foolish," she replies primly, but I hear a lightness in her tone that wasn't there when she was glaring down at me from her porch a minute ago.

We traverse through well-known paths back to my G Wagon and I open the door for her. She makes no comment about the vehicle, but then again, I didn't expect her to. That's not her thing… buying expensive stuff just because she can.

I put music on low and head away from Blackburn Farms. It only takes about five minutes of driving before I'm turning down a road that causes her head to turn my way. "We're going to the distillery?"

"Yup," I reply, shooting her a wink.

"It's a little late for a tour," she says.

"That it is and you really need to see it while it's operating, but I'm going to show you something else. Just be patient." She harrumphs and I ask, "How was Sylvie's day? I texted her and she said it was great but she was exhausted."

That keeps Kat occupied, telling me about horse camp, and by the time we're pulling into Mardraggon Distillery, the first manufacturing plant where our bourbon was created back in 1842, Kat seems more at ease.

We exit the vehicle and I take Kat's hand again. The parking lot is well lit, and surprisingly, she doesn't pull away. A security guard stands at the glass side-office door and moves to greet me as I use my keys to open it.

"Mr. Mardraggon, this is a nice surprise," he says.

"Hi, Marshall. I'm here to show my guest the tank."

"It's a beautiful night for that," the man says, bobbing his head.

"Indeed." Kat smiles at the guard and we move past him. I lead her down a maze of halls and then through an exit door at the back of the building.

We're immediately hit with the sound of gurgling water, compliments of a fresh water stream that meanders through the property. To the left is a large cylindrical metal tank with a steel ladder attached to the outside that extends all the way up. The roof is conical but not steeply pitched. A walkway fashioned around the top is bordered by safety railing.

"I seem to remember you're not afraid of heights," I say, sweeping my hand toward the ladder.

"No, I'm not, but that thing is tall enough you could throw me off the top and kill me," she replies tartly.

"Then I guess we'll see how much you trust me," I say, moving to the ladder and starting the climb. The tank is not overly tall, about eighteen feet high and twenty-five feet wide. "This was Mardraggon's first fermentation tank once we refined our process. It's no longer in use and just ornamentation now."

"Is it safe?" I hear from behind me and I can tell she's begun the climb.

"Very safe," I assure her.

I arrive at the top and step to the side on the walkway to give her room. I take her elbow to steady her as she moves from the top rung of the ladder. She ignores the railing, apparently secure in the belief I won't toss her over.

"Come on," I say, moving around the diameter until we reach the other side of the tank, and that's when Kat lets out a gasp of delight.

Stretched out below us is the stream and along both sides are hundreds of glass globe lights staked into the ground. They're of varying sizes and illuminate the grassy banks as the stream meanders around a copse of trees and disappears.

"What is that?" she whispers as I take her hand and point to the slanted roof for her to sit.

She does and I ease down beside her, stretching my legs and leaning back on my hands. "Alaine did that," I say softly, staring at the lights.

Kat's head whips my way. "She did? When?"

"A visit a few years ago. Sylvie was seven I think, and they'd come to visit me here at the distillery. Sylvie loved playing by the stream… hell, in the stream. She and Alaine would make picnic lunches and I'd go eat with them. Alaine was a stargazer and they'd come out here at night."

"A special place," Kat murmurs.

"I'd like to bring Sylvie here at night sometime, if it's okay with you. We'll figure a convenient time."

Kat's silent, drawing her knees up and wrapping her arms around her shins. "You can bring her on your own. You don't need me to chaperone. I'll work it out with Ethan."

I twist my neck to look at her. "Why the sudden change of heart as to my fitness as a guardian?"

Resting her cheek on her knee, she looks at me. "It wasn't sudden. It was proven over time and besides, I wouldn't be sleeping with you if I ever thought you could hurt Sylvie."

My hand goes to her back and I stroke it lightly. I don't know how much of the impishness she can see in my smile because it's dark up here. "And might I be sleeping with you tonight?"

"No," she says, her white teeth gleaming through the shadows and I hear the playfulness in her tone. "But perhaps tomorrow night."

Laughing, I scoot closer and wrap my arm around her. She surprisingly cuddles in, putting her head on my shoulder.

"I'm really sorry, Kat." I stare down at the lights and

wonder how to take her silence. Her body remains lax against me. "For what I did to you back then. I was a coward, but then again, you already know that. That's what you called me."

"I stand by that," she says softly.

"You're not wrong. I was back then. I let my parents' hatred and all I'd ever been taught to feel about your family cloud my judgment. I wasn't confident enough to evaluate and make my own decisions. I'm just… really sorry. I would change it if I could."

More silence but then she says, "You were a kid. We both were."

"I was old enough—"

"I'm thinking we both weren't ready for the repercussions of what would have happened."

"Maybe," I muse as I think about the hell that would've broken loose if we'd told our families. "Maybe not."

I think that Kat and I could potentially be married now with a family of our own had I been a bit braver. Sylvie could have cousins to play with.

We sit side by side, staring down at the lit stream and listen to the music of the running water. It's several minutes before Kat finally says, "I forgive you, Gabe."

I didn't know how much I needed those words, the release of weight on my shoulders making me feel like I could float off this tank. But I take Kat's hand and hold on, letting her ground me.

CHAPTER 20

Kat

I T'S LATE AS I walk to my Jeep, but there are plenty of streetlamps to light the way. Our board meeting ran late, mostly because we were having fun—eating good food and some of my fellow horsemen drank a little too much good bourbon—and I need to let Gabe know I'm on my way.

I stop on the sidewalk, rummage through my purse for my phone and shoot him a text. *I'm just now getting out. Going to run home and change. Be there in an hour.*

His response is quick and strangely warming. *Drive safe.*

It's crazy the turn of events in my life where Gabe is concerned. Since our talk on top of the tank the other night, we've easily slipped back into a relationship of sorts. It's reminiscent of what we had back in college in that we're both staying on the down low at my insistence, as things are just too precarious between the families and with his father's attempt on Sylvie's life, I'm not willing to throw things into disarray.

But it's also different in many good ways. We're more mature, settled and confident. That extends not just into the bedroom where sex is better than it ever was, but out of it as well. Our conversations are deep and we're exploring each other's lives. Things we were too young to care about back then are important now. For example, Gabe has opened up to me about how torturous this has been with what his father did to Sylvie. He never had a warm relationship with Lionel, but now he hates the man.

"I hate him more than I could have ever hated a Blackburn," he said last night as we ate dinner together. He then gave me a chagrined look. "Not that I ever really hated the Blackburns."

I laughed and assured him I understood what he meant. And I encouraged him to purge those feelings because who wants to carry around that crap. I also took the time to truly let him know how much it means to me and my family that he protected Sylvie and chose what was right over family ties.

We've spent every night together since our "tank talk," and I don't envision that changing much. I go over to his place though, as I don't want anyone seeing his vehicle at my apartment. Even if he were to park on the service road, I don't want anyone catching him making a predawn walk of shame.

Gabe doesn't want to keep things secret and I understand his desire to be fully open in his feelings. It's almost as if he wants to defy history and he's ready to take it all on, but I just can't right now. Not only do I want to keep the drama down with my family, but there's a small part of me that isn't fully trusting of Gabe. It's not an overwhelming fear and admittedly, I know deep down he's changed, but I can't seem to shake that tiny sliver of worry that he'll abandon me again. I'm guessing that's something I'll need to work through.

I pocket my phone and head down the block to the parking lot. There wasn't any street parking when I arrived at the restaurant in Lexington. I'm the president of our local professional horsemen's association and we meet quarterly. We do things such as help guide lawmakers in passing legislation, institute show rules and disburse the best information to horse owners, breeders and riders to promote horse health, safety and welfare. It's a fulfilling commitment and I've been involved in several equine organizations over my lifetime.

The parking lot is still half full. Although it's late by my standards—and I told Gabe I'd be done a lot earlier than now—it's still a young night in vibrant downtown Lexington. My Jeep is parked in the middle row and I wave to one of my board members as she exits the lot.

Keys in hand and my mind now consumed by thoughts of what Gabe and I will be doing once I get to his house, I get a prickling sensation on the back of my neck as I get closer to my vehicle.

Something feels off and it's nothing more than instinct as I look around the well-lit lot. I don't see another person and no obvious signs of danger, but still… my senses are causing unease within me.

I quicken my pace, unlocking my vehicle remotely so I can jump right in. Just as I reach for the door, I hear footsteps close by. I whirl around, my heart slamming against my ribs, just in time to see a man approaching me. He's big, dressed all in black, but the most alarming thing is that he has a black mask over his face.

There's no spike of fear or instinct to bolt as I realize I'm about to be robbed. I mentally prepare to hand over my keys and purse, knowing he most likely wants an easy score. I'm going to give it to him with no fight but those hopes are dashed when a black Suburban pulls up behind my Jeep. The man in the mask doesn't even look at the other car, which tells me whoever is driving behind those tinted windows is no friend of mine.

He moves with terrifying efficiency, lunging so fast, I drop my purse and keys as my hands instinctively come up to ward him off. One strong hand is behind my neck and the other clamps over my mouth, stifling any scream I might think to utter. It all happens so fast and I'm so terrified, I'm frozen to inaction.

Leaning close to me, he growls, "Don't you dare fucking scream or I will end you."

That seems to knock me out of my paralysis and I reflexively scream against his hand but it's muffled and doesn't carry. The man's hand grips my jaw hard, causing so much pain I feel like it's going to fracture, and tears spring to my eyes. But now my sense of self-preservation has ignited and I kick him hard in the shin. Grunting in pain, his hand loosens its grip, but before I can scream, he crosses his arm over his chest and lets a backhand fly at me. It catches me high in my cheekbone, hard enough I stumble, one leg slipping out from under me. My knee cracks into the pavement but I ignore the pain, intent on running.

I don't act fast enough though as he grabs me by the hair and painfully pulls me up, and when I'm eye to eye with the man, I freeze again as I see the end of a pistol hovering in front of my face.

"Now," he says softly but with such ice in his words, my bladder threatens to release. The overhead streetlamp throws most of his face in shadow, but I see he has light blue eyes that are as frosty as his demeanor. "I'm only going to say this one time. You get in that Suburban quietly and politely, and you won't get hurt."

"Why are you—"

Crack.

He backhands me again. Same hand, same cheek, but I don't go down. "Let's try this again. You are to be quiet. That means no talking. Are we clear?"

"Bellamy," a voice says from behind my attacker and I realize the driver's door has opened to the Suburban. Another man dressed all in black with a face mask steps out. "Don't hit her again."

Fury flashes in those blue eyes and I can see he doesn't like being told what to do. Just as I can see he likes hurting people… maybe even has an affinity for women in particular. Grabbing my upper arm and squeezing so hard I can feel it in my bone, he flings me toward the other guy. The driver catches and steadies me from falling and I note he has soft brown eyes.

If I thought that would make him nicer, I'd be wrong because he also warns, "Don't make us hurt you. That's not our objective but we will if necessary. Do you understand?"

I blink back tears welling from fear and the pain in my cheekbone, the edge of my eye starting to swell. I nod, afraid to utter a sound.

"Good," he says, escorting me to the back door of the vehicle. He opens it, urges me in, and the monster with the blue eyes follows me. He sits placidly, staring straight ahead as his partner gets back behind the wheel. I'm mute, frozen solid, but I can't tear my eyes off the gun that rests casually across my captor's thigh with the barrel pointed at me.

My mind races, every scenario I can imagine more terrifying than the last. *Who are they? What do they want with me?* My thoughts spiral, desperately searching for a reason but finding none. I've never been involved in anything that would lead to this—nothing that makes sense.

Are they serial killers? Rapists? If they're masked, maybe that means they won't kill me since they're keeping their identity secret. Strangely, that one thought gives me hope.

I'm a good girl, keeping utterly still and my mouth shut as we traverse the streets of Lexington. The two men don't talk so I can't glean any clues as to what they want and I'm too petrified to ask. Instead, I focus on my breathing, trying to quell the panic that claws at my throat. I've read about situations like this in the mystery thriller books I love. I've seen them in movies. Stay calm. Observe. Remember details. But nothing prepares you for the cold, hard reality of being snatched from your life by masked strangers.

They make no effort to conceal where they are going and this ratchets up my terror again, because dead people can't give away locations. We leave Lexington, jump on I64 East which takes us straight to Shelbyville. Are they from my hometown? Are they taking me home? Going to kill me in my home county?

But we pass by Shelbyville and drive straight for the heart of Louisville.

Although I'm a Kentucky native and I've been to

Louisville many times in my life, I don't know it all that well. We navigate unfamiliar city streets into a rather seedy area, making so many turns I'm completely lost. Finally, the driver pulls up behind what looks to be an abandoned warehouse. Everything is dark, no working streetlights and no people around. The perfect place to do dark deeds.

The men waste no time dragging me from the vehicle, the blue-eyed guy pressing the gun to my back so that I behave as requested. I'm so scared he's going to pull the trigger accidentally that I barely pay attention to where we're going. It's a cavernous building that appears to have once been a manufacturing facility but it's completely empty now. Just worn brick walls and dusty concrete flooring. An interior light glows weakly at the far end in what appears to be a room with a large window that overlooks the plant floor. I imagine that's where the facility manager probably worked, the glass cut out in the wall so he could make sure things were running smoothly.

I'm guided in that direction, neither man saying a word. When we reach the office, I'm ushered inside and the blue-eyed monster the other man called Bellamy steps in with me. The brown-eyed man says, "I'm going to park the car."

His partner doesn't reply, merely pushes me over to an old metal desk with a chair. With a hand on my shoulder, he shoves me down into it.

"I'll be right back," the brown-eyed man says, and I can hear a slight tinge of worry in his voice. "Do not touch her while I'm gone."

Bellamy says nothing and instead sits down on the corner of the desk. His gaze falls on me with the weight of Thor's hammer and I'm forced to look away. I can't tell who has seniority in this partnership but he's not taken to task for his failure to respond, and then the brown-eyed man is gone.

I watch as he melts into the darkness of the warehouse, the light on in the office and lack of illumination beyond making it a pitch-black blanket of unknown. It makes being stuck inside here with this monster that much more terrifying because I don't know which is the bigger danger. Somehow, I think I'd prefer to be in the dark, not knowing what's lurking behind me, than sitting with this asshole who likes to hurt people.

CHAPTER 21

Gabe

G LANCING AT MY watch, I see that Kat's now twenty minutes late, but I don't let it upset me. She's never been extremely punctual in casual situations. I give my attention to the layout on the coffee table. A critical once-over and I deem it romantic enough. Fresh flowers, strawberries and a bottle of chilled wine. I thought Kat and I could hang out on the couch for a bit and talk, but not for too long. She has an early day tomorrow, as do I, and I'm going to need time in the bedroom before we go to sleep.

I'm helpless not to smile when I think of how far we've come in the last few days. It's been a slog just being able to have a civil conversation with her, but the tide has turned and there is finally a bright spot in my future. After all the heartache from Alaine's death, to losing Sylvie to the Blackburns, to my father's perfidy, I've somehow come out of this with a gift.

I don't intend to take it for granted or waste it either.

My phone rings and I pull it from my pocket. I don't recognize the number so I send it to voicemail. It's almost certainly related to work and I'm officially off the clock. Ordinarily, I'd answer, but with Kat due here any moment, I'm putting work behind her.

I barely have it slipped back in my pocket when it rings again.

Same number.

I'm irritated at the intrusion and the audacity of someone to call back, especially when they're not even known to me as they're not in my contacts. I again push the call off to voicemail but within moments, it's ringing again from the same number.

A prickle of unease coats my skin in goose bumps that turns into dread. What if it's a hospital calling that something has happened to one of my parents? Or God forbid, Kat.

That thought has me stabbing at the button to connect the call. "Gabe Mardraggon," I answer brusquely, hoping beyond hope this is a work call.

"I want my 1921 Shadow Reserve, Mr. Mardraggon."

It's a male voice, deep and mature. I don't recognize it and yet I know exactly who it is. "Then I'm afraid you're out of luck, Mr. Rafferty. As I told your goons, it's not mine to give and even if it were, I'm not going to help my father."

"Yes," he says with a resigned sigh. "We realize there's no leverage in your father. But perhaps you would help another loved one?"

I frown at that cryptic statement and the incoming chime of a text has me pulling the phone away from my ear with morbid curiosity. It's a text from the same number and with dread, I enlarge the tiny thumbnail of a photo the caller sent.

When it is full screen, my breath evaporates in my lungs, leaving me speechless and struck by insidious fear.

It's Kat, sitting in a chair with a black cloth tied around her eyes. Behind her stands a man wearing a black ski mask and he has a gun pointed at her head. I can't tell if he's one of the original men who paid me a visit, but it doesn't matter.

Kat's in trouble.

My voice quaking with fury, I bring the phone back to my ear and snarl, "You fucking son of a bitch. I'm going to kill you for this."

"No, you won't," Rafferty says brusquely. "In fact, I expect you'll do exactly as I say. You're going to get the case of bourbon and I'm going to text you an address to bring it to. You give me the bourbon, I give you the girl. It's a win-win situation."

"And if I choose to just call the police?" I ask with contempt. "I've done my research on you and you're a fairly upstanding member of Louisville society. Surely you don't want this becoming public."

Rafferty laughs, clearly amused. "Do that, and you won't see your precious Kat Blackburn again. And good luck proving I had anything to do with this, but in the end, it won't matter. You won't have the girl and I'm willing to roll the dice that you're not going to risk a hair on her pretty head."

He's not wrong about that. The bourbon doesn't mean shit to me. Twenty seconds ago, it was part of my family's legacy, but right now it's just brown liquid in dusty bottles. "I want to talk to Kat right now."

"Sadly, I have to decline, Mr. Mardraggon." He sounds so smug and I want to knock his teeth down his throat. "But you have my word she is safe and un-harmed. Bring me the case of bourbon, don't involve the police, and you'll have your girl back in your arms before you know it."

"She'll be there when I bring the bourbon?" I ask to clarify the terms.

"Yes. We'll switch out, easy as pie. You walk one way, I'll walk the other, then we forget this happened. I don't think I have to impress upon you how driven I can be when I set my mind on something, so if you think to involve the police or try to fuck this up in any way, I will ensure the people you love suffer. And just so we're clear, I'm not talking about your parents but rather a cute little girl who looks an awful lot like your girlfriend."

Not my girlfriend and at this moment, I regret ever reconnecting with Kat. Had I kept my hands to myself, kept far away from her, this douchebag wouldn't know she means anything to me. He's clearly connected and has done his research—my best guess is I've been followed from the moment they first approached me and they've had plenty of opportunity the last two weeks to see the time Kat and I have spent together. Hell, Kravitz probably saw me kiss her at the gala.

Fuck, I hate myself for putting her in danger, but it never crossed my mind that she would be targeted. Hell, I didn't take this Rafferty prick seriously anyway because who does shit like this for a case of rare bourbon?

Regardless, it's his liquor now and I'm going to bring it to him. I'm also not going to involve the police because he's now threatening Sylvie and if paying my dad's debt makes everyone safe, I'll do it without a backward glance.

"Where do I make the delivery?"

"Louisville," he replies. "I'll text the exact address."

"I'll need two hours but if you hurt her, I will destroy you."

"Relax, Mr. Mardraggon. She's perfectly safe and will remain that way as long as you bring the bourbon."

"You have a fucking gun pointed at her head," I growl in rage at the bastard. "I don't call that perfectly safe."

"Time's a ticking, Mr. Mardraggon. I'll text the address."

The line goes dead and I don't waste a single moment. I blow out the candles I'd lit and I'm out the door, taking my G Wagon because I need more room than what the Ferrari offers.

It's not to collect the bourbon first though.

I head out to Blackburn Farms.

♦

KNOCKING ON THE front door, I glance at my watch. It's almost nine thirty, about fifteen minutes since I hung up with Rafferty. The lights are ablaze in the Blackburn ancestral home but I've never darkened this doorstep before.

I hear the sound of laughter from inside and then the door opens. Ethan has a wide smile on his face, clearly leftover from the laughter still echoing in a nearby room but it melts off the second he sees me.

Or rather, my expression, because he immediately asks, "What's wrong?"

"Is Sylvie here?"

"Yeah… she's sleeping." He throws his thumb over his shoulder. "We've been hanging out with Marcie, my parents and my brothers playing cards."

I grimace because the thought of having to deal with all the Blackburn brothers is not appealing but there's no time to worry about that. I'm just glad Sylvie's not around to hear this.

"Gabe," Ethan barks, no trace of humor left from his family card night. "What's wrong? Is Sylvie in danger?"

"No, it's not Sylvie. It's Kat."

"What?" Ethan exclaims, and he starts to step out onto the porch.

"Your entire family better hear this," I say, holding up a hand. Ethan halts but doesn't invite me in. His indecision irritates the hell out of me. "It's fucking urgent, Ethan."

That seems to jar him and he scrambles back from the door. I push past him, following the sound of voices with Ethan hot on my heels. I find myself stepping into the kitchen where I find Fi, Tommy, Wade, Trey and Marcie sitting around the table with playing cards scattered about.

They freeze when they see me, Wade's mouth actually hanging open.

It's Trey who breaks the silence, his gaze going to Ethan who comes to stand beside me. "What's this knucklehead doing here?"

"He's here about Kat," Ethan says.

"She's at a meeting in Lexington," Fi says in her Irish lilt. "Then she was going out with friends after."

I shake my head. "She's in trouble." Christ, this is hard... I don't even know where to start, but I can't seem to start with the most important thing—that I love her. Instead, I launch into the story from the beginning, talking at breakneck speed to get it all out because every minute delay is another minute that Kat is sitting there in terror. "My dad was apparently gambling and bet a very rare case of bourbon in a game of poker. He lost and the man who held the marker sent some goons to try to collect from my dad. Except, it's not his bourbon to give. It belongs to the company, so they came to me for collection and I refused. But they want to force my hand, so they kidnapped Kat tonight—"

"What the ever-loving fuck?" Ethan yells at me, both of his hands going to my chest and he shoves me viciously backward.

I take the stumble but correct myself, eyeing him warily. Every other Blackburn plus Marcie rise from the table in alarm. "If I take the bourbon to him, he'll let Kat go. I'm on my way right now to get it, but I had to let you know what was going on. They said she's safe and unharmed and they'll let her go as soon as I bring them the case."

Fiona takes a step forward, her voice soft and surprisingly calm. "I don't understand... why would they be takin' Kat?"

"And why would that matter to you?" Tommy says, his voice sounding like barely contained violence as he comes to stand beside his wife.

"Because we're seeing each other," I say, holding Tommy's gaze. Say what you want about her having three overprotective brothers, it's her father I owe the explanation to.

"Bullshit," Wade says with a wave of his hand, not believing such a thing could happen.

I don't have an opportunity to convince him because there's a blur of movement and then Trey crashes into me. He drives me into the wall but I manage to brace against him so the impact isn't too hard. His fist rears back as I grab a handful of his shirt, preparing to return the hit, but then we're being pulled apart.

Tommy and Wade each have one of Trey's arms and Ethan puts a restraining hand against my chest.

Trey's face is red with rage. "I'm going to kick your ass for even thinking you're good enough to breathe the same air as Kat."

"Get over yourself, asshole," I bark at him. "Kat is being held against her will in some strange place and she must be terrified. You can try to kick my ass after we get her back, but I have to go now. I just wanted to tell you what was going on."

"We should call the police," Marcie suggests.

"No!" I shake my head. "They warned me not to involve the police and if I did, not only would Kat be hurt, but they'd come after Sylvie. I don't know if it's a bluff, but I'm not risking it. I'm taking the bourbon to them and they said they'd release her."

"I'm coming with you," Ethan says.

"Me too," Wade grunts, letting go of Trey's arm.

"Fuck if you're leaving me behind," Trey adds, his eyes glacial as they lock onto me.

"And I'm going too," Tommy says.

"I figured you'd all want to come but someone needs to stay here with Sylvie," I say, turning to face Tommy. I have a feeling he's going to be the decision maker. "My suggestion is Ethan comes with me and everyone else stay here with Sylvie."

"I don't like this," Fi says, her hands wringing. "Maybe we should consider the police."

I struggle to remain calm, forcing myself to take a breath and I soften my voice. "Mrs. Blackburn… please don't risk Kat's life like that. Their instructions are clear and I'm gladly willing to give up that bourbon. If that gets Kat back safe and keeps Sylvie safe, that's what we need to do."

"I agree," Ethan says, and his brothers nod, although Trey makes a show of cracking his knuckles. Not sure if that's for me or Kat's kidnappers. "Where's the bourbon?"

"In secured storage at the distillery. It won't take me but a minute to get it and then I've been texted an address in Louisville to take it."

"Then I suggest you get going," Tommy says.

"You should bring weapons," Wade suggests.

"I don't think that's a good idea." I had considered it myself but quickly abandoned it. "I really think all the man wants is the bourbon and then it will be over."

I don't dare tell them I was sent a photo of Kat blindfolded with a gun to her head.

"Are you sure?" Ethan asks with worry. "Because I don't want to go to a gun fight without a gun."

"Yeah… I mean, I'm pretty sure."

Trey launches himself at me again but his dad and Wade intercept him. He screams at me over their shoulders. "You better be sure, asshole. That's my sister's life."

"Weapons won't be needed," I grit out.

"Are you absolutely certain?" Ethan demands again and I get why he is pushing the point, but I'm out of goddamned patience.

"The only thing I'm fucking sure about is that I love your sister, okay? I'm going to get her now. You can come if you want but no weapons."

Once again, the room goes deathly silent as everyone stares at me slack-jawed by my admission. But it's Trey who breaks it by lunging again. "Going to kick your ass."

I don't let Tommy or Wade stop him, instead meeting him head-on. Both my hands grip his shirt and I drive him backward now, right into the counter. He grunts in pain as his lower back—hopefully his kidneys for extra enjoyment on my part—collides with the edge. "I don't have time to deal with your bullshit. You can be a baby about this or you can man up, but I don't have time to dick around with you."

I release my hold on Trey and spin away from him, not concerned at all that he might attack. I saw his own fury change into chagrin when I called him a baby.

"I'm leaving. Ethan… are you coming?"

"Yeah, and I agree. Trey and Wade should stay here with Dad."

A small argument breaks out among the brothers, the younger ones not wanting to be left behind. I don't wait for them to figure it out but by the time I make it to the front door, Ethan's the only one at my side.

Once we're in my vehicle, I note the whole family standing on the front porch watching us. Tommy holds his wife close, Marcie beside Fi holding her hand. Wade leans back against the doorframe, a worried look on his face. Trey stands with fists clenched, looking like he wants to murder me.

Kat has a lot of people who love her and what do you know… that includes a Mardraggon.

I'd prefer silence between me and Ethan but he has too many questions as I drive to the distillery and I can't say I blame him. I just dropped some bombshells and this has to be immensely shocking to him.

"Go over again the chain of events and how this

occurred," he says.

"A little over three weeks ago, not long after my dad was removed as chairman of the board, two men showed up at my house. They told me my father had been gambling with their boss… a man named Clinton Rafferty… and he bet a case of our 1921 Shadow Reserve in a high-stakes poker game."

"And lost," Ethan says.

"Not only lost, but refused to pay up. So Rafferty sent his goons to try to scare me into giving it up."

"Scare you how?"

"Threatened me, went and roughed up Lionel—"

Ethan turns in his seat, his words crusted with ice. "And you didn't think that would put Kat in danger?"

I glance at him briefly before turning my eyes back to the road. "Kat and I weren't together then."

"Wait a minute," Ethan huffs with frustration. "When exactly did you and Kat start seeing each other?"

Hmmm, that's a difficult question to answer but I might as well spill the entire truth. "Our freshman year at UK."

"What in the hell?" Ethan exclaims and then rubs the bridge of his nose. "You were… back in college… but she never said anything."

"Because I wanted to keep it secret." I let that sink in and Ethan picks up on the regret in my voice.

"And she didn't. She wanted to be open about it," he

surmises.

"And we broke up because I was an idiot. Caught up now?"

"No, I feel like I'm spiraling down the rabbit hole," Ethan mutters. "But you reconnected when…" His words trail off and then he curses angrily as he puts it all together. "When I asked her to handle the winery with you. Goddamn it."

"Yes," I drawl sarcastically, shooting him a glare. "It's all your fault."

"No," he snarls. "It's all yours."

"No," I snap back at him, refusing to take the full blame. I can have regret, sorrow and anger that this has happened, but I didn't cause it. "This is Lionel's fault, but you know what… it's your fault too. And your parents, and brothers, and Kat's, and mine, and every other idiot ancestor we have. This stupid fucking feud that's been egged on by generations of hate and I'm sick of it. It cost me the girl I loved eight years ago and once we get Kat out of there, I'm not going to let it interfere in my life again. So you and your numb-nut brothers need to get on board with the fact that Kat is mine and our families are tied together now, even more than Sylvie bound us."

I brace for a blast of righteous indignation from the man but he stares out the window and I enjoy the silence.

At the distillery, I enter through the same door I brought Kat through a few days ago, a different security guard meeting us and waving us on. Ethan follows me through the mash house portion of the plant, the sweet, cereal-like aroma washing over me. Ethan eyes the large grain mills and mash tuns where we mill the corn, rye and barley down into grist before mixing it with water. It goes into the tuns to convert the starches into fermentable sugar, and from there, it goes to an annexed building and into huge fermentation tanks.

We don't go that way though, instead exiting out the back of the mash house and walking across the campus. We pass the distillation units and finally approach the aging plant which houses row upon row of charred oak barrels, stacked ten high on shelves. This building is different from the others in that in addition to requiring a key to get in, it requires a passcode. These barrels are the epicenter of our business and the most valuable part of the plant, so they are protected with the highest security.

I punch in the code and we enter, moving down the center aisle of the long brick building with concrete flooring. At the end is another door with another security panel that requires a different passcode, this one known only to me and my Uncle Terrance. My father used to have it but I changed it the day he was ousted.

I press in the nine digits that unlock the door and

glance at Ethan watching with interest. The door opens to an anteroom that has a table with two leather chairs to sit in but what causes Ethan's eyes to bug out is the massive steel door before him. It's as large as those used in bank vaults and just as secure. It requires my thumbprint to unlock and then I spin the large wheel to slide the bolt free. I pull the heavy door open and flip on the light.

"Whoa," Ethan says as he takes in the custom-built wooden shelves that hold a variety of steel lockboxes. On one side of the room is a large bookcase stacked with leather-bound journals, records of all the bourbon production from the time our doors first opened in 1849. Other boxes hold important documents regarding the Mardraggon empire from land grants, trust agreements, contracts for sale and even some prenup agreements that were used down the generations. There are even some old diaries and letters, all perfectly preserved as this room is temperature and humidity controlled.

None of that interests me now because it's the case of 1921 Shadow Reserve I'm after. It's on its own shelf along with a handful of other rare bourbons. While the Shadow Reserve is our oldest, it's not the only one worth money. However, I'd give up every single case right now to get Kat back because it suddenly seems silly to have such things sitting in here accumulating age with no enjoyment.

I snag the case off the shelf and turn to Ethan. "Let's go."

He hasn't said a word since we set foot on the property and I see a million questions in his eyes. I can tell he's interested in the plant, the processes and all the secrets this room holds, but now isn't the time.

We have more important things to do.

CHAPTER 22

Kat

I HAVE NO clue how much time has passed and while I expected the cruel man named Bellamy to fuck around with me, he's been strangely quiet. I can still feel his ominous presence though, and every once in a while, he leaves the small office we're in.

I only know this via sound because when the brown-eyed man came back from parking the vehicle, I was blindfolded and zip-tied to the metal chair. While the plastic ties aren't overly tight, I can't help but struggle against them. My skin is chafing, so I try to hold still.

I can't see anything but a thin haze of light at the bottom of the cloth tied around my face, and my cheek throbs from the two backhands I received. I don't need a mirror to know it's bruised and swollen because I've taken enough falls from horses to know what such abuse does to my body.

Try as I might, I could not get either man to answer my barrage of questions once the blindfold went on. My first one I asked tentatively, afraid I might get hit again. "Why are you doing this?"

"Because we can." This was from Bellamy, his voice deeper and more gravelly than his partner, his words sneered with contempt. I can only glean he's a woman hater with the small bit of knowledge I have.

But the other man added, "It's not for you to worry about. If everything goes according to plan, you should be released soon."

"If everything goes according to plan?" I echoed. "What does that mean? Why am I involved? What's this really about? Am I ransom for something, because my parents have money and will give whatever is needed to get me back? If you let me make a call, I'm sure I can speed things up."

Neither one answered and it made me more desperate. My voice was nearly hysterical. "Please tell me something. Anything. Are you going to hurt me? Is this retaliation because if so, I don't deserve this."

Something hard pressed against my head and I knew instantly it was a gun. Bellamy spoke close to my ear, punctuating his words, "Shut. The. Fuck. Up. Or. I. Will. Shoot. You. In. The. Head."

"Enough," the other man barked and the gun was gone. It fell silent in the office, but I was scared enough to keep my mouth shut.

Since then, I've had time to think of all the good

things waiting for me in my life. My family, my horses, my sweet little Sylvie.

Gabe.

I wonder what he thinks that I never showed up to his place tonight. There's a part of me that worries he'll take it as a blowoff and this tenuous relationship we've tried to reestablish will be shot all to hell. He'll learn differently once he finds out I've been kidnapped.

More than likely, Gabe is going to be worried. I'm assuming my phone is still back in Lexington near my vehicle where I dropped it. I expect he's probably tried calling but has enough time passed that he'd call the police? Would he potentially call my parents or Ethan? If he did that, it would expose our relationship and that's not something I want.

But I don't want to be kidnapped either. I don't want the threat of rape or death hanging over my head because it's done nothing but cause a constant roll of nausea in my belly and heart-pounding fear in my chest. I think I'd gladly take Gabe exposing our relationship if it meant the police will be storming in here to rescue me.

Except… how will they know where I am? I have no clue why I'm even here because my captors have frozen me out.

I mull over their reluctance to talk or show me their faces, and the best I can figure out is that they have no intention of being caught. They are limiting my knowledge and the more they keep secret from me, the more hopeful I am that I'll come out of this alive.

The door rasps open and I listen intently to the scuff of shoes across concrete flooring and then the closing door. My ears strain to pick up anything and I believe I'm alone.

Not that it is of import, because I've dutifully followed the order that I keep my mouth shut. I try to roll my shoulder, aching from the position I've been sitting in. I twist my wrists slightly and wince at the rub of the zip ties against my tender skin. I stretch out one leg, then the other, and try to shift on the hard seat because my ass hurts. My cheek hasn't stopped throbbing and the pain has overtaken my entire head in the mother of all headaches. The intermittent bouts of tears I've shed haven't helped at all and my throat is so parched, I'd kill for a sip of water.

The door opens again and I freeze a moment before cocking my head that way. Footsteps approach and I tense but then someone is cutting my ties free. My inclination is to bolt but instead, I force myself to remain calm and merely rub at the tender skin.

"Your boyfriend has come to get you." I recognize the voice of the brown-eyed man.

My mind reels from his words because why in the world would Gabe be involved in my kidnapping? Why would he be the one to pay the ransom?

The blindfold is lifted from my face and the light is too harsh, so I'm forced to squint against the blinding glare.

"Let's go," he says, taking my upper arm to guide me out of the office.

At the far end of the building where we entered I think a few hours ago, I see the rolling doors have been pulled wide and three vehicles sit parked, headlights on. It bathes that end of the warehouse in light, but the men standing there are silhouetted. The closer we get though, I can see Gabe's G Wagon and it's as my captor said… my boyfriend has come to get me. A large SUV looks like the one we rode in to get to this place and next to it is a black Mercedes sedan with dark tinted windows.

There's no rush of joy or relief though, because it can't be as simple as Gabe bringing something in exchange for me. I was freaking kidnapped off the street at gunpoint, beaten and then threatened to be shot. These are dangerous men and I can only hope Gabe knows exactly what he's dealing with.

Someone gets out of the back seat of the Mercedes and I squint the closer we get, trying to make out the figures. The wash of illumination from the headlights hurts my eyes after being blindfolded for so long.

"There she is," the man from the Mercedes says, but I can't see the details of his face due to the searing headlights. I raise a hand up as a partial shield, hoping to cut some of the glare so I can see who's talking. "Safe and sound. Do you have the Shadow Reserve?"

"I have it," Gabe says, and my head whips that way. A figure moves toward me and I notice another one walking beside him. Gabe and…

My jaw drops open as I make out my brother Ethan. What in the hell is going on? I want to scream at everyone standing here but I don't forget these men are armed.

Gabe comes to stand before me, his eyes locked on mine for a moment as if trying to convey a message. I think it's assurance and that makes me feel marginally better but then his gaze drops to my cheekbone. His hand cups me under my chin, turning my head so he can get a better look, and his jaw hardens.

He doesn't turn to face the other men but grits out, "Who hit her?"

"I did," Bellamy confesses with actual pride in his work and Gabe looks over his shoulder. I can see him standing there but the mask is off now. He's got short-cropped hair, those glacial eyes and a sneer on his lip. I note the brown-eyed man also has his mask off now. He has blond hair, but he looks no kinder, not the way I'd made him out to be.

"Let's make the exchange." This from the man who exited the Mercedes. He's just a middle-aged, average-looking man in a business suit. "You got the girl, now give me the bourbon."

"Bourbon?" I say in confusion.

Gabe's attention comes back to me. "I'm so sorry this happened but you're safe now."

Leaning down, he presses his lips to my forehead and then takes my hand. He leads me over to Ethan and says, "Watch her."

I'm dumbfounded and utterly confused as Gabe moves to the G Wagon. He opens the rear door and walks back around holding a case of what I'm assuming is bourbon… Shadow Reserve they called it?

He sets it down on the ground though and looks at the man in the suit. "You said she'd be unharmed, Rafferty. But your guy hit her. Bruised her. That can't go unpunished."

Tugging his cuff down, the man clasps his hands before him. "So I did. What did you have in mind?"

Gabe rolls up his shirt sleeves and then removes his watch, shoving it down into his pocket. "I want five minutes with your guy."

My head whips toward the man who hit me and he remains stone-faced, awaiting his boss's direction.

"No," I exclaim and try to move to Gabe, but Ethan holds my hand tight. Gabe doesn't even glance at me, his eyes pinned on the man he wants a piece of. I turn to Ethan and hiss, "What the hell is going on?"

His green eyes meet mine and I see censure in them.

"We have a lot to talk about. But later. I want to watch Gabe kick this guy's ass."

"Very well," the man named Rafferty drawls in an attempt to sound cultured yet slightly annoyed. He looks at Bellamy and jerks his head toward Gabe. "Please avail yourself to Mr. Mardraggon."

Without a word, Gabe and Bellamy square off. Gabe's body is taut as the blue-eyed man circles him, fists raised. The headlights throw stark shadows, making the scene feel more like a duel than a brawl. Bellamy lunges, throwing a heavy punch aimed at Gabe's head. Gabe dodges to the left, and I gasp as Bellamy's fist passes just inches from Gabe's face.

Counterattacking, Gabe throws a quick jab that connects with his opponent's jaw, but it's a light touch, a warning. Bellamy sneers, wiping his mouth, and charges again. This time he's faster, his large fist catching Gabe off guard and landing a solid hit against his cheek. I cry out and squeeze Ethan's hand hard, fearful of what might happen.

Gabe stumbles backward but recovers quickly. Rolling his shoulders, he waits for Bellamy's next move. He's overconfident and charges without thought. As he comes forward aiming for another heavy blow, Gabe steps inside his reach, delivering a sharp uppercut to the man's stomach. It knocks the wind out of him, and he doubles over.

Not giving my attacker a chance to recover, Gabe grabs the back of the man's head, pulling it down as his knee comes up, striking the man's face. Blood spurts from his nose, causing him to roar and swing wildly. Gabe easily backs away from the sloppy attempts to strike him.

When Bellamy lurches upward and throws his fist, Gabe blocks the clumsy effort and delivers two rapid strikes, one to the kidney, another to the ribs, each hit precise and forceful. The thug cries out in pain, his body curling defensively. Gabe steps back, watching as the man struggles to maintain his footing and it would be a good time to walk away. But Gabe isn't done.

With an almost gleeful look of determination, Gabe advances on Bellamy, now panting heavily, his face etched with misery and smeared blood. I watch astonished as Gabe throws a series of hard, fast punches, targeting the head and body, each strike delivered with fury and protectiveness. The man tries to retaliate, but his punches are slow, easy for Gabe to sidestep.

Finally, with a powerful right hook, Gabe sends the man crashing to the ground, unconscious. Standing over his fallen opponent, Gabe breathes heavily, his fists still ready, his body primed for more, but the fight is clearly over and I wonder if he feels vindicated in some way. I know that I didn't mind watching, now that it's all said and done.

Gabe reaches into his pocket and pulls out his watch. As he fastens it back on his wrist, his gaze moves to Rafferty. "I assume we're done and that I won't see your guys anymore."

Rafferty smiles and steps forward, hand outstretched. "Pleasure doing business—"

"Fuck off," Gabe growls and nods down at his man on the ground. "Or else I'll put you right down beside him. If I see you or your men anywhere near me or mine, I'll throw the full power of my empire behind destroying you."

The smile slides from Rafferty's face and he flushes red. With a curt nod, he says, "Understood."

Gabe, Ethan and I stand still as Rafferty gets back in the Mercedes. The blond goon helps Bellamy up from the ground and they leave in the SUV. It's only then that a long, pent-up breath is released and my shoulders sag.

"Let's get you home," Ethan says, his arm around my shoulders. He pulls me into his side protectively, guiding me toward the G Wagon, and I know he's sending Gabe a message.

I pull free from my brother's grasp and move to Gabe, who oddly hasn't come near me. He stands with his hands loose at his sides but he looks like he's ready to blow into a million pieces. I glance down, see blood on his knuckles and reach for them to inspect, but he steps back.

I shake my head, censure in my tone. "Don't do that. Let me see your hands."

"I almost got you killed," he growls. "Not quite worried about my hands."

Ethan steps forward, touches my shoulder. "Come on, Kat."

"No," I snap, rolling my shoulder so his hand's thrown off. I step in close to Gabe, tipping my head to look up at him. "What was all this about?"

"Paying a debt my dad owed," he grits out. "He bet a case of rare bourbon and I refused to give it to Rafferty. They took you, so yeah... my fault I almost got you killed."

"You couldn't have known they would kidnap me," I scoff.

"Doesn't matter," Gabe says, heading around the front of the G Wagon. "Ethan's right. Let's get you home. Your family will want to see you."

It doesn't take a rocket scientist to know Gabe is riddled with guilt and while I want to have a long talk with him—to thank him for rescuing me and to work through his feelings—I can't do it with Ethan in the car. I also don't feel like getting into it with my brother as I know the inevitable argument will come about me seeing a Mardraggon. So I wait and bide my time.

The ride back to Shelbyville is utterly silent. Ethan chose the front seat, forcing me into the back, and as I sit on the passenger side, I study Gabe's taut profile, his jaw locked in anger. His gaze seems a million miles away as he drives us home.

When we pull up to my family's house, the door is flung open and everyone—except Sylvie who I assume is sleeping—pours out. Ethan texted them on the way home I was safe and next thing I know, I'm out of the vehicle and being passed around for hugs. It's a whirlwind, being hugged, kissed, twirled and looked over critically by my mother who insists on getting ice on my face.

The sound of Gabe's vehicle reversing gets my attention and I jerk away from my mom. Gabe is actually turning around to leave.

Without talking to me.

Without saying goodbye.

Without some type of explanation as to what happened, not just tonight but where we stand right now.

I run over to his SUV as he's still in reverse, slamming my hands down on the hood to glare at him through the windshield. His expression is inscrutable as we engage in a staring contest.

"Just let him go," Wade calls out, but I don't budge an inch.

"It would be good fucking riddance," Trey mutters.

"Don't," Ethan growls, and I jolt slightly at the anger in his tone, but I don't take my eyes off Gabe. "He got

Kat back safe at great cost to himself and on top of that, he kicked the shit out of the man who hit her."

"Let's go inside," my father says and that surprises me. I would put him firmly on Team Hate Mardraggon with Trey and Wade. And despite how my dumbass brothers act all overprotective, it's my dad Gabe should fear.

He's letting me handle this on my own which doesn't necessarily say he trusts me, but rather… he must trust Gabe to some extent. It's probably sunk in the way it has with Ethan, that he went to great risk tonight. Probably personal expense too, as I have no clue what that case of bourbon was worth, but enough to warrant a kidnapping.

From the corner of my eye, I can see my family moving toward the porch and once they're inside, I move around to the driver's door. To my relief, Gabe puts the vehicle in park and exits.

"What are you doing?" I demand. "Why would you leave without saying anything or talking to me about this?"

Gabe sighs and rubs a hand over the back of his neck. His gaze slides over to the house and lingers there a moment before returning to me. "My family has done some fucked-up things to yours the last few months. I thought maybe you and I could have something, but tonight is just further proof that the Mardraggons are toxic to your family. I'm toxic to you."

"You're not—"

"You could have died tonight," he barks at me, face contorted in anger. "They sent me a fucking picture of you with a gun to your head. That guy was completely unhinged and this could have ended very badly. As it stands, you were hurt, and I'll never forgive myself for that."

"Good," I yell back at him. "Don't forgive yourself because you did nothing wrong. This was all on your dad."

Shoulders sagging, he shakes his head. "Doesn't matter... it was still a Mardraggon and babe... I'm still a Mardraggon. Some things just run too deep to be overcome."

"Bullshit." I point my finger back at the house. "Why was Ethan with you?"

He blinks in surprise at the question and I think he's so off guard, he doesn't seem to consider sheltering the truth. "Because they deserved to know what had happened to you. They had a right to help decide the best course of action."

"Which meant you had to tell them about us," I surmise.

"Yes," he clips out. "I had to tell them and I'm sorry. I know you didn't want me to."

"No, I wasn't ready, but guess what... cat's out of

the bag now, and you and I are still standing here talking without my brothers or dad trying to kill you. We did it. We made it past that horrible hump of telling my family that a Mardraggon and a Blackburn are going to try to make a go of it."

"None of that matters, Kat. We aren't good together. Our families aren't good together."

"Historically, yes… our families are oil and water. But you and I… we are good together."

Gabe's eyes shutter and I can see him refusing to accept that. Just as I see the resolve filtering in and a glint of Mardraggon ruthlessness sparking. "We're good together in bed and that's it. That's not enough to overcome all that's bad."

"You're wrong," I assert.

"I'm not and you know it."

"Gabe," I murmur, reaching out for him, but he turns his back on me. I stand my ground, refusing to beg. It reminds me of the way he hurt me back in college, the abandonment of a different sort, but no less stinging.

He pauses a moment and twists his neck to look at me over his shoulder. "I'm going to remove myself as co-trustee for Sylvie. I think Ethan is capable enough with your help to manage the winery issues."

"And that cuts our only tie to each other," I say bitterly.

Gabe doesn't say anything, just stares at me with pain-filled eyes a long moment before stepping into his vehicle.

Before he shuts the door, though, I get the last word in. "So you're abandoning Sylvie too? Just going to cut her out? You forget… she's also a Mardraggon."

Gabe visibly flinches and I can see that hadn't crossed his mind when he was making such grandiose statements that our families can't mix. He doesn't reply because I don't give him a chance to. I let him chew on that as I spin on my foot and head to the house.

I hear his car slip into gear and he drives off.

In the foyer, my mother awaits me. She takes my hand and pulls me toward the kitchen. "Come on, luv. Let's get ice on your face and a nice cup of tea, shall we?"

I tug back but not overly hard. "Sounds heavenly but honestly, I just want to crawl into my own bed and sleep."

My mother ignores my reticence. "You can sleep in one of the guest rooms here. I'll stay with you," she insists, her Irish field eyes sparkling with unshed tears of worry. I can't disappoint her need to care for me.

"Okay, Mom. That sounds good."

I let my mother fuss over me as everyone settles into the kitchen to listen as Ethan explains how the entire thing went down. Marcie sits beside me, patting my leg periodically. I downplay what happened to me to keep further worry to a minimum, but the entire time, I'm fretting on the inside about Gabe. He had the guts to tell my family we were together when he didn't have to include any of them in this. He could have brought the bourbon, secured my release and it would've been our secret. But he told my family. They had the right to weigh in on how the entire situation would be handled and I appreciate that more than he'll ever know.

Without a doubt, he's at least secured Ethan's complete respect. My brother told me as much as I sipped my tea and held a bag of frozen peas to my cheek.

But Gabe left without giving any credence to what we've rebuilt together. The stubborn part of me says I'll fight to keep Gabe and I'll hound him until he relents.

However, the part of me that still remembers the first time he hurt me feels very tired and unsure. That part is telling me to let this go and move on.

It's telling me to remember that Mardraggons and Blackburns do not mix.

CHAPTER 23

Gabe

D RAGGING THE BACK of my hand across my forehead, I grimace at the gritty dust and sweat that comes off. A shower can't come soon enough but I'm bound and determined to finish this last set of shelves.

Oddly, for a man who's used to sitting in bespoke suits behind a desk, I'm getting a lot of satisfaction from the backbreaking work of organizing our storage vault.

The idea didn't come to me out of the blue as I've been wanting to get in for years to root around in the ancestral documents and collectibles. I've always been so proud to be of Mardraggon lineage and there's a wealth of history in this room. But while I've always wanted to do this, it was clearly never a priority. I never seemed to have the time and what little free time I did have, I didn't want to be doing sweaty physical labor like this.

But it's exactly the type of activity that seems to bring me some measure of peace. Because when I'm concentrating on my work here—going through boxes, organizing, cataloging, moving them—I'm not thinking about Kat.

It's been three days since I dropped her off at her home with the intention of leaving her firmly behind. As of now, I'm sticking to it.

Doesn't mean I didn't waver though, especially that very next day when Kat showed up on my doorstep as I was getting ready to head to the office. She caught me off guard, moving into me to place a blistering kiss on my mouth.

One I'm ashamed to say I returned for way too long before I got ahold of myself and pushed her gently off. She tried to step into me again and damn her to hell, she whispered dirty words. I knew her game though… get me in bed and she could talk to me after she had me boneless from pleasure.

I knew if I let her get me into bed, my resolve to stay away from her would crumble, so I did the only thing I could.

I lied to her and I did it cruelly. "I'm not interested, Kat."

She narrowed her eyes, motioned to her body, slamming in a pair of short shorts and a tight T-shirt. "You're not interested in this."

Christ, it killed me and I almost couldn't pull it off, but I managed to keep my tone unaffected. "It was good while it lasted but it's run its course."

I braced for her to fight or at the very least slap me, but instead she looked at me with sad eyes. "Still the same asshole you were eight years ago."

She turned and walked off. I watched as she got into her Jeep and drove away. I wanted to scream at her that I wasn't that same asshole and that what I was doing was to both our benefit, but I stood mute as her taillights disappeared down the drive.

I'd like to say each day has gotten easier, but it hasn't. So I'll continue to work long hours at the office, leaving my father's legacy behind and building my own. I'll spend my nights working through the storage vault, not once regretting the empty space where the Shadow Reserve used to sit because I'd have given up this entire company to make sure Kat was safe. Then I'll go home too exhausted to think and fall into a dreamless sleep that has been my sanctuary for the last three nights.

"Excuse me, Mr. Mardraggon."

I turn to the vault's open door to see a security guard there. We employ several to walk the campus at night, which covers over four hundred forty acres.

I don't recognize this one but that's not unusual. I'm not typically here at night and rarely during the day, my work being conducted from the Frankfort offices. "What's up?" I ask, once again wiping a bead of sweat threatening to roll down my temple.

"There's a Mr. Ethan Blackburn here to see you."

I glance past the guard's shoulder and see Kat's brother standing there. He raises a hand tentatively. "Sorry to come unannounced."

Sighing, I wave him in and thank the guard, who slips away unobtrusively. "What can I do for you?"

"Well, you'd know if you bothered to answer my calls or texts," Ethan says as he walks over to a shelf of collectibles. He picks up an old paperweight, examines it and sets it back down gently. "Why are you avoiding me?"

"Because I'm not going to discuss your sister with you," I reply, moving back to another set of shelves where I'd emptied a box of documents to sift through. I thumb a few pages but I can't concentrate on them. However, if I ignore Ethan long enough, maybe he'll leave.

"I want to discuss Sylvie," Ethan says, and that gets my attention.

I glance at him as I point out, "I thought my email to you day before yesterday was clear. I'm going to have myself removed as co-trustee so you don't need to have my approval on anything."

"I'm talking about working out some type of visitation schedule with you," Ethan replies.

I turn to face him fully. I'm still skeptical, but I ask, "What type of visitation?"

"The kind where she visits with you. Spends time.

THE FORBIDDEN

I'm even comfortable with her doing an overnight or flying to France again."

I bark out a laugh and shake my head. "Nice try, but if you're using that as a ploy to get me and your sister back together, then forget it."

"No ploy. Kat doesn't need to chaperone. I trust you with my daughter."

And once again, he has my undivided attention, but I can't let the skepticism go. "You trust me? Are you addled or something?"

Ethan chuckles. "Yeah, yeah... I know. You're a Mardraggon and I'm a Blackburn, and our families have hated each other for eternity."

"Exactly," I say, stabbing a finger in the air at him. "So pardon me if I'm a little suspicious of this sudden change in attitude."

"Not sudden," Ethan corrects me. "It had been happening from the start because it's always been clear you love Sylvie. It only compounded when you turned your dad into the police, and hell... by the time you were giving up a two-million-dollar case of bourbon to save my sister and then stomping the ass of the guy who hit her, I was pretty much ready to welcome you into the family."

Shaking my head, I turn away to focus on the sheaf of papers before me. "You're full of shit."

"I'm not," Ethan says, but I keep my back to him. "I

277

trust you and if you want time with Sylvie, you have it. And I know you don't want to hear it, but it bears saying… I think you're wrong to let my sister go."

I don't reply.

"You said you loved her. Told my entire family in our kitchen. Was that all bullshit?"

I swallow hard, wanting to lie to him but I can't. Keeping my attention on the task before me, I have to admit to him, "No, it wasn't bullshit."

"Then why the fuck aren't you over at the barn right now begging her forgiveness and getting on with the business of being happy?"

"Because I'm a Mardraggon and she's a Blackburn."

"Because you're too afraid to be a Mardraggon and love a Blackburn," Ethan sneers. "You're not your father, you know?"

"I know."

"You're not responsible for his debts or his actions."

"Got that too," I mutter.

"So you're just being stupid then." Ethan laughs and it's mirthless. "Maybe I shouldn't trust such a bonehead with Sylvie."

I turn on him, angry at the words he's saying but appreciating them all the same. "You know I really hurt your sister eight years ago."

"She told me all of it," Ethan says, and I don't miss the menace in his voice.

"I hurt her again just days ago."

"Your point?" Ethan drawls, crossing his arms over his chest.

"Don't you think it's just a little reasonable that I back away and let Kat have a shot with someone who's better than me? Someone who's guaranteed to give her what she deserves?"

Ethan shakes his head, a small smile playing at his lips. "Life doesn't come with guarantees. It's all about risk and reward. Yes, you might face more challenges. Yes, it's going to be hard with the family feud still simmering. But don't make decisions based on fear. You and Kat, you have something real. You owe it to yourself and her to see where it leads, without shadows from the past dictating your future."

Christ, I hate that what he's saying makes a future with her seem plausible. I hate it because I never thought a Mardraggon would have to rely on a Blackburn to make sense of life. That's twisted in a way I don't want to consider.

"What's your sister think about all this?" I ask. Because surely he's had this same talk with her. She's been stubbornly silent since she left my house three days ago when I spurned her advances.

Ethan tips his head back and laughs. As his eyes meet mine, he looks almost sorry. "Dude… she is pissed at you. I'm not sure you can win her back."

"What the fuck, Ethan?" I snarl. "Why did you just lay all that bullshit on me?"

"Not bullshit, my friend." Ethan claps me on the shoulder and squeezes. "And I do mean that. After everything, you are my friend. Now, Kat is a different story. It's going to require much groveling."

He turns and moves to the door. I stroke my jaw in contemplation, wondering just how much groveling it will take.

"Oh," Ethan says as an afterthought, his hand on the vault door. "Trey and Wade very much are not on board with this and that's up to you to work out. They still want to kick your ass for what you did to her in college."

"Of course they do," I mutter, but honestly… it would be a small price to pay.

Not to mention, I probably deserve it.

"Catch you around," Ethan says. "Maybe at a family dinner or something."

His laughter echoes inside the vault as he walks away and that's just not something I can see in the future.

Me sitting at the family dinner table in the Black-burns' home.

But I can see me begging Kat to give this a shot and that's where I need to start.

CHAPTER 24

Kat

T HE LAST RAYS of sun paint the sky in a riot of
oranges and pinks, casting long, dramatic shadows
across the sprawling fields of Blackburn Farms. The air is
cool, a welcome relief given how hard I've worked today.
Rather than give lessons, I worked the horses, which
included several lunge sessions as well as rides. I even had
a quick spin on Shadow around the outdoor paddock.
He got a little frisky, gave me some buck, but nothing
that even came close to knocking me off.

Now all is quiet. The horses are fed, the last of the
staff have gone home for the night, and the final thing
I've got to do is shut and lock the massive rolling doors
on the east end of the facility.

The south wall of the barn has pop-out windows that
are open a few inches and through them I hear the
crunch of gravel just outside, indicating a vehicle is
pulling up. Most likely Ethan on his way from the
yearling barn to try to entice me into coming to dinner

but I'm not feeling like it. I'll politely decline, he'll tell me to get my head out of my ass, and we'll devolve into a yelling match.

Last night I was so mad at him because he was trying to extol Gabe's virtues and I didn't want to hear any of it. Twice now I've wasted my time on that fool. So yeah… last night I most definitely didn't go up to the main house for dinner and instead went home, showered, uncorked a bottle of wine and called my twin, Abby, to vent to her.

She's a good sister so she patiently listened with lots of supportive and affirming words, and when I'd run out of steam after two glasses of wine, she told me I needed to work things out with Gabe.

I called her a traitor and hung up on her, but later sent her an apology text. Her reply was as dry as the wine. *I'm sure it was the alcohol talking.*

I don't veer toward the office to intercept Ethan. He can just wait in there for me. I continue my journey through the freshly dragged dirt, thanks to a few trips around the arena with the rake attachment on the back of the UTV. That's usually done first thing in the morning by one of the stable hands but I don't mind doing it. I mean… who doesn't love zipping around on a UTV? I might have cut some doughnuts down at the free end where I do lunge lessons, but it was all good because I smoothed it out after.

I pull both doors closed and flip out the lights at the end of the barn. One of the horses nickers and another launches a kick at his stall door. I smile, loving the sounds of my life.

Turning to head to the office and gearing up to battle it out with Ethan, I come to a dead halt when I see Gabe standing there. He came into the barn area through the office door and his presence charges the air, thickens it with things unsaid and feelings unsorted. He stops a respectable distance away, his hands buried deep in the pockets of his jeans, his posture rigid, as if bracing for a storm.

"What are you doing here?" I ask, crossing my arms over my chest and glaring at him, although secretly… I suppress a chill from how beautiful he looks. His hair is windblown and while he can rock a suit, I prefer him in denim.

"Can we talk?"

"Sorry," I reply as I head toward the office, which means I'll have to walk by him. "I'm late for family dinner."

His hand shoots out, latches onto my wrist. "Five minutes, Hell Kat."

I don't let him goad me. Instead, I glance down at his hand but he doesn't remove it. When my eyes meet his, I pointedly remind him, "You weren't interested in talking last week when I came to your house."

"You weren't there to talk," he counters with a wicked grin. "You were there to seduce me."

I jerk my arm away from him. "Maybe, but I wanted to talk after."

"I'm here to talk now," he replies softly and with such yearning, my heart squeezes. Just that easy, he knocks the wind out of my sails. The angry banter and bitter jabs that would prevent any meaningful discussion don't seem appealing right now.

"Fine," I say with a sigh. "What do you want to talk about?"

"I want to talk about us." His expression is guarded, and I can tell he's afraid of saying the wrong thing. "About our future."

"A future that I've twice tried to have with you and you've run scared both times," I say acidly.

"I ran scared once," he corrects, his eyes blazing with indignation. "The second time, I was doing you a favor."

"Are you stupid or something?" I ask incredulously.

Gabe's hands fly outward in exasperation. "Yes, I'm stupid. I thought that all the crap between our families and my father continually fucking things up—trying to kill Sylvie and almost getting you killed—meant that you were better off without me. That you would be happier. But I've been told recently that line of thinking is idiotic."

I narrow my eyes on him. "Ethan came to see you?"

"Yeah, last night. He didn't tell you?"

I shake my head, marveling that my brother would take a stance. My entire family has been quiet on the Gabe issue, but I think they're all afraid to bring it up.

"He came by to tell me that I could see Sylvie… without a chaperone."

"Oh, wow."

Gabe nods, a soft smile playing at his lips. "He said he trusted me. Called me his friend."

"Really?" I ask with wide eyes. "He said that?"

For a minute, I forget all about the problems Gabe and I seem to be facing and marvel at what a monumental step this is, not just from Ethan who is incredibly protective of Sylvie but who has more reason to hate the modern Mardraggon family than anyone.

I have to say… it's impactful that Ethan trusts Gabe.

"I think I made an impression on your brother," Gabe says.

I nod in understanding. "Turning your dad in. Rescuing me. I imagine that goes a long way with Ethan."

"I think it was more walking into your family home and telling everyone that I loved you."

His words hit me hard because no matter how good we had it for a short period eight years ago, neither one of us ever uttered that phrase. And maybe that's why we didn't work out back then because we weren't ready to give our hearts completely.

The implication of what it means now is staggering. "You told my family you love me?"

"It didn't go over very well," he mutters. "Trey wanted to kill me."

"Trey's a hothead. But you really said that?"

Gabe steps into me, hands going to my face in a move purely to hold me captive. Forcing my head to tip back, he bends closer and his eyes fall on me with the weight of a hammer. "I love you, Kat. It started eight years ago and while it might have faltered, the feelings never stopped. Over the years, I always felt the loss of you and the sting of regret. And so many horrible things have happened… Alaine dying, losing Sylvie to your family, my father turning out to be a wacko. But fuck if I can really bemoan any of that right now because without all those things happening, you and I would have never been given a second chance. So I choose to be grateful for the opportunity and yes, I fucked it up a bit this past week, but I've always been a bit slow to process feelings. I have to digest things and I have to learn how to put myself out there. That's what I'm doing… putting myself out there right now to you.

"I'm telling you that I love you and that I want to have a life with you. I want our families to support us on this and we might have to work hard to get it to happen, but it's time to let the past go—for everyone. If there's ever a reason for everyone to get on board with that, it's

Sylvie. She deserves to have her family completely united and whether your family likes it or not, Ethan has opened the door to me. And I'm walking through."

It's a good thing he's got me secured with his hands because I've never had my knees go so weak just from words.

But no… not just words.

That was a statement.

A mantra.

An oath.

A creed.

My throat tightens with emotion, but I manage words of my own. "How could I not love you after that?"

"Is that a rhetorical question?" he asks, the corner of his mouth quirking.

"Yeah… shouldn't be a question at all. I should give the same affirmation. I love you. You've shown through words and deeds that your character and heart are bigger than anyone could have imagined. I'm glad it didn't take any longer for me to see it because I don't want to waste another moment of this life without you."

Gabe exhales so visibly, he almost curls in on himself but then his mouth is on mine and he's kissing me so deeply that he becomes part of me. And in that touch, a new dawn rises for us both, one that is free from the past with the unspoken promise that we'll only look forward. We're going to make our family do the same, not just for our sakes but Sylvie's as well.

Our mouths part and he briefly brushes his lips on my forehead. "We have work to do on your family."

"At least Ethan's on our side," I reply, wrapping my arms around his waist and pressing my cheek to his chest. The steady thump of his heart is reassuring.

"And Sylvie," he adds. "She's on our side."

"And I'm pretty sure my mom is too. She's Irish and a romantic at heart."

"The rest is a piece of cake," he says with a chuckle, and I can't help but laugh. It's not going to be easy getting Trey and Wade on board but the one thing I know, Gabe is ready for it. He's taken control of his life, cut out the toxic portions and bravest of all, faced down my family in a high-stress situation to tell them he loves me.

There's nothing that can stop us now.

CHAPTER 25

Gabe

U PON OPENING THE storage container, the musty smell of old paper and leather fills the air, almost overpowering the scent of the aged oak barrels that line the walls just on the other side of the open vault door. Sylvie is at a small table we'd moved in here, her head bent over a journal she's reading.

I grin at her, not able to stop myself from teasing. "How come I'm doing all the manual labor and you're over there lollygagging?"

She doesn't even look up at me. "Lollygagging? What type of word is that? Sounds completely made up."

I pause to consider and shrug. "No clue but it means not doing the task you're supposed to do."

Which I don't mind. I'm just glad Sylvie wants to spend time with me in here and more importantly, that Ethan held true to his word and let her come. While Kat or any other Blackburn isn't required to be here to watch over us, I'm disappointed Kat isn't here. But she's got work to do at the farm, which has been something I've found mildly difficult to acclimate to.

Now that we're in the open, have declared deep feelings and have some family approval, I just want to spend all my time with her. If I had my way, I'd give her a job as my secretary, just so she could sit outside my office and I could stare at her all day long, but I realize that's a ridiculous fancy. Besides, I could never take away her work because she loves it so much and it just so happens my girl is a hard worker.

We've settled into a routine where we take the time given us, mostly in the evenings where I'll stay at her apartment or she'll come to my house. We've not yet ventured into a family dinner at the Blackburns, although in fairness, Fi has invited me. But Trey is still being a bit of an ass to Kat, insisting she's making a mistake and of course, I think he's a moron.

"He needs to let it go," Kat muttered last night as we lay in bed.

"Well, it's like a hundred and seventy years of hate between the families," I pointed out, feeling the need to give her brother some leeway. He's only protecting her after all.

She scoffed at the notion. "It's got nothing to do with the original feud. He's pissed about us seeing each other in college and the way we split apart then."

"Oh," I murmured, because that's a bit harder to

overcome. I hurt his sister back then—I'd want to kick my ass too. "Maybe he and I should just go at it. Let him get it out of his system."

Kat sat up in bed, the sheet falling to her waist, and I had a hard time focusing with her glorious nakedness shining back at me. Her hand on my chin, forcing my gaze to her face, did the trick. She was smirking but I could also see a hint of worry. "I saw the way you destroyed that asshole who hit me week before last. You beat him to a pulp and I'm sure my brother would come out on the losing end."

"I'd let him win so he feels better about it."

Kat's eyes softened at the gesture—which I was very serious about—and kissed me gently. Then deeply, then the conversation was forgotten.

Sylvie's excited voice from the other side of the room pulls me back to present. "Gabe, come look at this!"

I set aside the bin I'd just opened and walk over to the table where she's camped out. Our goal for today is just to catalog all the historical journals and other documents that have been kept in climate-proof boxes. I figured it was a good way to give Sylvie some of her heritage so she doesn't forget the good part of her Mardraggon blood.

Her eyes are wide, finger pointing at a page filled with tight, looping script that at first glance looks impossible to read it's so small.

"Listen to this entry," she says, her voice trembling with anticipation. She clears her throat and reads aloud.

June 15, 1852

It is with a heavy heart and a burdened soul that I commit these words to paper, for I am compelled by a force stronger than my own will. My affection for Elizabeth Blackburn, a jewel amongst the common stones of our town, has driven me to actions unbecoming of a gentleman. Yet, what choice have I when faced with the prospect of her union to Henry Mardraggon, a man unworthy of her grace and beauty?

This evening, under the shroud of twilight, I found myself at the old tavern where whispers travel faster than the wind. There, amidst the shadows, I let slip a tale most foul, yet necessary. I spoke not with malice but out of a desperate desire to sway her heart toward mine. The rumors of her alleged indiscretions—an invention of my own making—are designed to cast doubt where there should be none. With doubt, surely Henry will call off the impending nuptials.

As I lay these words down, I am tormented by the dual nature of my actions. Is it not a man's right to fight for his heart's desire? Yet, how can one justify the tarnishing of an innocent's reputation in pursuit of personal happiness? The very ink that stains this page is a testament to the conflict that wages within me.

I pray that the morrow brings clarity and, with God's grace, forgiveness for my transgressions. My only solace is the hope that once free of her ties to Henry, Elizabeth will turn her affections toward a man who loves her truly and deeply.

May time prove me a fool for my actions and restore the honor of the lady I hold in such high esteem.

I frown as Sylvie looks up at me. "Who wrote that?"

Holding her place on the page she just read, she closes the journal to show the name *Tommen Mardraggon* embossed on the front. "I don't know who that is," she says, "but he's confessing to starting the rumors about Elizabeth Blackburn."

"You know the backstory?" I ask.

Sylvie nods, eyes still pinned to the confession. "Papa told me."

The name Tommen Mardraggon isn't familiar to me, but I know where I can find the answer. I move to a bookshelf that has an old family bible where our family tree had been filled in by some distant relative.

I open it up and adjust slightly as Sylvie sidles up next to me. The lines of lineage take up two pages and I find Henry Mardraggon's parents and start skimming from there down, following branches as they extend outward.

"Here it is." I tap on Tommen Mardraggon's name. "He was a third cousin to Henry."

"And apparently in love with Elizabeth. Does that entry mean he did that on purpose to break up Henry and Elizabeth?"

"It seems that way," I muse, moving back to the journal. I open it to the front and see many entries dating back a few years from Tommen Mardraggon. He worked in our distilling business as a manager of sorts and mostly liked to write short poems and fiction. But I found several odes to Elizabeth who apparently only had eyes for Henry.

Jesus... he didn't just ruin Elizabeth's reputation, he put into action the feud between the families, causing the accidental death of Henry and inciting Elizabeth to take her own life.

I flip past the entry Sylvie just read and there are a few more. She and I read them, basically an accounting of the gossip that started to spread through the town and Tommen's plan to step in to restore Elizabeth's honor when she was ready. But then the entries stop abruptly and while I don't know the exact date Henry was killed, I'm guessing that's when Tommen stopped writing. I would have expected someone callous enough to come up with this lie so he could get the girl to take advantage of Henry's death, but maybe he had an attack of conscience.

I'm not sure we'll ever know.

"That's good though," Sylvie says, and I look down at her in question. "I mean… we know that Elizabeth wasn't unfaithful and that someone set her and Henry up."

"A Mardraggon set them up," I reply, struggling to keep my tone unaffected, although I can almost taste the bitterness. Just one more strike against my family and now I have to wonder if this will reignite the feud.

"What's with the long faces?"

A thrill zips through my body at Kat's voice and Sylvie and I both turn to find her walking into the vault. She's wearing a pair of faded jeans, muck boots and a T-shirt. The least fancy outfit one could put together, but she looks like a million bucks. Her long black hair is tied in a loose braid that hangs over her shoulder with tendrils of hair that have come loose.

I move to her, put a hand to one hip and give her a light kiss. "What are you doing here?"

"Thought I'd come see if my two favorite people wanted to get lunch. Just so happens… I brought a picnic and thought we'd eat down by the stream."

My eyes cut to Sylvie whose face lights up with joy. That was a thing with her mom and now it's going to be a thing with us. "Awesome. What did you bring to eat?"

Kat shakes her head. "Nope. Not another word until

you tell me why both of you looked sad and pensive when I walked in."

Sylvie and I exchange a glance before I take Kat's hand and lead her to the table. Sylvie moves to the side and I point at it. "Your niece found a journal written by a Mardraggon cousin back in 1852. He is the one who started the rumors about Elizabeth because he apparently wanted her all to himself. He intended to break up the wedding with Henry and was going to swoop in to claim her."

"Really?" Kat says, eyebrows shooting high with interest.

"Right here," Sylvie says, pointing to the entry.

Kat bends over the book and runs her finger above each line as she reads it. When she's finished, she straightens and shrugs. "He sounds like a total idiot. Okay, so I brought fried chicken and potato salad, hot from Miranda's miraculous hands."

"Yum," Sylvie exclaims. She has acclimated very well to southern food.

"Wait a minute." I'm so perplexed, I find myself actually scratching my head. "That's it? He sounds like an idiot?"

Kat frowns at me. "What did you want me to say? He's an asshole?" Her gaze cuts to Sylvie. "Sorry for the language." Then back to me. "Because yeah… sounds like an asshole."

I shake my head, befuddled. "Kat, you get that this places the blame for all of it solely on a Mardraggon. Before, it's just been a lot of finger-pointing but this is proof that Elizabeth and Henry would most likely have married. None of this feud would've ever occurred if not for my family."

She shrugs again. "I guess… but what does it matter? It's stupid. That happened so long ago, Elizabeth's and Henry's bones are probably dust by now. The idiotic thing was for subsequent generations to carry that bitterness forward. I mean… look at us. We were taught to hate each other and we both did, without there even being a good reason for it. It's ridiculous if you ask me."

"You might feel that way, but others won't," I point out. "Once this becomes common knowledge—"

Kat takes the book, closes it and hands it to me. "My suggestion is you put this back where you found it and forget about it." She turns to Sylvie. "What do you think?"

Sylvie also shrugs. "Think about what? No idea what you're talking about."

Kat laughs and pulls Sylvie in for a one-armed hug. "That's my girl. Now let's go eat. I'm starved and I have to get back to the barn soon."

Giving her niece a push toward the vault door, Kat says, "Grab the basket sitting out there and we'll meet you at the stream."

"Okay," Sylvie chirps, waving as she leaves.

I'm still reeling from the discovery and from Kat's blasé attitude, but I really am dizzy when she steps into my arms and presses her mouth against mine.

Not just her mouth but her entire body, which causes mine to react. I savor her kiss for a moment, her soft curves, before I break away. Christ, she turns me on with the simplest of touches. "Need to save that for tonight," I chastise.

Kat grins at me, eyes sparkling. "Only because Sylvie's expecting us. But if she weren't here, you best believe we'd be closing that vault door and handling business."

Laughing, I take her by the hand and we head out to join Sylvie. "I love that about you. And you're sure we should keep this new knowledge from the rest of your family?"

Kat loops her arm through mine as we walk along the rows of aging barrels. "I don't think it's relevant. It certainly won't do anything to pave a smoother road between you and the rest of my family."

"No, it won't," I muse before turning toward her, stopping us just before we reach the door that leads out. A few workers mill about, but no one's paying us attention. "You're being very protective of me and what we're building."

"Of course I am," she replies. "I want this to work."

"It is going to work," I growl, leaning in to steal a kiss. "I'm not letting anything stand in our way."

"I love that about you. Your commitment."

"Took a while to get there," I mutter, touching my forehead to hers. "But I'm here… with you… all the way."

Kat tilts her head, our lips in contact again, but it's only a soft brush of our mouths against each other. "All the way," she whispers her agreement. "All the damn way."

The Bluegrass Empires series continues in November 2024 with *The Tryst*! Trey Blackburn isn't one to get tied up in a long-term relationship, much preferring the one-night kind of relations. But Trey's hesitation to commit might be deeper than not wanting to put in the time and effort. His reluctance may have more to do with the blonde beauty who just blew back into town and the things they left in the past that have been neither forgiven nor forgotten. GO HERE for details on The Tryst (Bluegrass Empires, Book #3)!
https://geni.us/SB_TheTryst

Go here to see other works by Sawyer Bennett:
https://sawyerbennett.com/bookshop

Don't miss another new release by Sawyer Bennett!!! Sign up for her newsletter and keep up to date on new releases, giveaways, book reviews and so much more.
https://sawyerbennett.com/signup

Connect with Sawyer online:

Website: sawyerbennett.com

Twitter: twitter.com/bennettbooks

Facebook: facebook.com/bennettbooks

Instagram: instagram.com/sawyerbennett123

Goodreads: goodreads.com/Sawyer_Bennett

Amazon: amazon.com/author/sawyerbennett

BookBub: bookbub.com/authors/sawyer-bennett

About the Author

New York Times, USA Today, and Wall Street Journal Bestselling author Sawyer Bennett uses real life experience to create relatable stories that appeal to a wide array of readers. From contemporary romance, fantasy romance, and both women's and general fiction, Sawyer writes something for just about everyone.

A former trial lawyer from North Carolina, when she is not bringing fiction to life, Sawyer is a chauffeur, stylist, chef, maid, and personal assistant to her very adorable daughter, as well as full-time servant to her wonderfully naughty dogs.

If you'd like to receive a notification when Sawyer releases a new book, sign up for her newsletter (sawyerbennett.com/signup).